COUNCIL

Serving Yo

LIBRARY

TELEPHONE: 01634 337799

Books should be returned or renewed by the last date stamped above

THE HEART OF HEATHERTON HALL

When the village school where she works is threatened with closure, Polly takes a part-time job waitressing at Heatherton Hall. Once a hive of activity, she discovers its decline is down to the questionable practices of the manager. As she becomes friendly with the owners, who have strong links with the school, Polly is determined to put things right. With the help of the handsome but troubled gardener Steve, she cooks up a plan.

ANNE PACK

THE HEART OF HEATHERTON HALL

Complete and Unabridged

LINFORD
Leicester

First published in Great Britain in 2023 by
D.C. Thomson & Co. Ltd.
Dundee

First Linford Edition
published 2024
by arrangement with
the author and
D.C. Thomson & Co. Ltd.
Dundee

*A catalogue record for this book is available
from the British Library.*

ISBN 978–1–4448–5382–7

Published by
Ulverscroft Limited
Anstey, Leicestershire

Printed and bound in Great Britain by
TJ Books Ltd., Padstow, Cornwall

This book is printed on acid-free paper

Village School

Polly rode her bicycle slowly between the children in the playground, their excited squeals as they chased each other almost drowning out their calls of 'Hi, Miss Wilson.'

She smiled and raised a hand then dismounted at the bicycle shed which was much more sophisticated than the one she remembered from her own school days.

A few mums and dads hung around the gate as usual, taking the chance to catch up with each other in this sleepy little hamlet.

Inside, Polly hung her jacket and helmet on a coat hook and shook her head to free her hair.

Through the glass partition separating the entrance hall from the office she could see Marjory, the head teacher, talking to teacher Clare.

Polly got on really well with both and knew that they made a formidable team

1

as they helped each child to realise their own potential.

She had been quick to appreciate the valuable difference the teacher-to-pupil ratio could make.

'Good morning,' Polly greeted them now. 'Anyone for a cuppa?'

She filled the kettle from the jumbo-sized bottle of water they kept for that purpose.

'Morning, Polly. I've already got one, thanks.'

Marjory held up her mug with her initial on the side. She was on the computer, checking e-mails. She shared with Clare the teaching of the school's 18 pupils.

Clare also held up her full mug from where she stood at the window watching the playground activity.

'Is that a new bike, Polly?' she wanted to know. 'Or did I dream your bike was blue yesterday? The one you rode this morning is red.'

'Well spotted. Yes, it's a new bike. Well, new to me. It's Izzy's cast-off. She's gone and bought herself the latest model and asked if I'd like her old one.

'I didn't need asking twice — it's in much better nick than mine!'

The distance from Polly's home in the town of Dalcleish was roughly three miles but it was amazing the saving she made on fuel by cycling instead of driving, plus she felt all the better for the fresh air and exercise.

'Talking of Izzy,' Polly continued, 'it's her birthday next week. Any ideas on what to give the woman who has everything?'

Aunt Isobel was her mum's much younger sister and had always been more like a fun big sister to Polly.

Izzy had never married, had a vibrant social life and loved being outdoors.

After the usual suggestions were thrown around — a voucher for a spa treatment, silk scarf, cycling gloves — Marjory held up a hand.

'Didn't you say your aunt was a keen gardener?'

'She is but I'm not sure she'd appreciate yet another pot plant,' Polly replied with a frown.

Marjory drank the dregs of her coffee and stood up.

'Actually, I was thinking more like a season ticket to the gardens at Heatherton Hall. I've seen the scheme advertised in various places. I thought about getting one myself, in fact.'

Polly thought, then nodded.

'That's a great idea; I think she'd like that. I'll check online later. Thanks, Marjory.'

'Right, let's get the day started.'

Marjory reaching for the hand bell.

Clare headed into the main room which was divided into two classrooms by a set of folding doors that could be pushed back along a track to make one big space.

The bell sounded and the noise level in the playground subsided as the children gathered around Marjory.

Polly could picture the scene, the ringing of that same hand bell as other teachers had done down the years.

The photographs high up on the walls

bore testament to that history.

The children soon settled at their desks and Polly took the register and lunch orders. These she sent off to a local woman who prepared the food at home and brought it in to the school.

As Support For Learning Assistant, Polly sat in on lessons, helping where needed.

Two of the pupils in the younger class needed a little extra assistance which warranted her services.

Both were delightful children from loving families. Polly often went home overflowing with a sense of satisfaction after overcoming an obstacle with one or both of them.

Today was no exception. For the first time Tommy managed to read the word on every single flash card. Polly's gentle persuasion and encouragement had paid off.

She was still grinning from ear to ear when she pulled on her outerwear at lunchtime, ready to go home.

Marjory beckoned her into the office,

unnerving Polly by the serious look on her face. She sat at her desk and clasped her hands.

'I'll tell Clare this news later but I feel it's only fair to tell you before you go home. I've just heard that the school is under threat of closure — again.'

Polly gasped but before she could speak Marjory put her hand up to silence her.

'We've lived under such a threat for years, as you may know, and have always been reprieved.'

After a pause she continued in a lower tone.

'This time I'm not so sure, however.'

Polly could feel the morning's joy slip away.

'The pupil numbers have been gradually dropping over the years and in a few weeks we'll lose another three pupils who will go on to high school,' Marjorie went on.

'Aren't there younger children due to start?'

Polly had only been employed here

for 10 months so she wasn't fully in the know about the local families.

'We have one. The younger sister of a current pupil.'

A horrified thought struck Polly.

'The school will close this summer?'

'Not this year. We've been told unless things pick up there will be no alternative but to close next summer.

'The locals will fight it tooth and nail, of course, like they always do.'

The older woman leaned over and touched Polly's hand in a motherly way.

'Heatherton Primary has been here for over 150 years, since it was built for the children of the workers at the Hall. Take heart and hang on to that thought.'

Polly cycled home in a daze. She hadn't been sure at first about working in a rural school after a bustling inner-city one, but now the thought of having to leave its tranquillity filled her with sadness.

Aunt Izzy

'Afternoon tea for two at Gleneagles, no less!' Izzy whistled on reading the voucher that was tucked inside the card.

'Thank you both so much! You know how to treat a girl. I'll ask one of my friends to go with me. We'll make a day of it.'

'So you should,' Polly's dad, Jim, agreed.

Polly hoped Izzy wouldn't be too disappointed to get yet another voucher but she needn't have worried. If anything her response was even more effusive.

'How thoughtful! I haven't been to Heatherton Hall for years. There used to be so many things going on there at one time. I went to basket-weaving classes. Thank you, darling.'

Izzy put an arm around her niece and kissed her cheek.

They were sitting in the dining-room of Polly's parents' house which had unfettered views of the surrounding countryside.

Polly had driven them for a change. It made sense since they lived near each other and it meant Izzy could have a glass of wine after their meal.

Her exuberant aunt always had a tale to tell so the journey had been entertaining and a good distraction from the worrying news of earlier.

'Happy birthday to you!' Fiona, Polly's mum, started off the singing.

She presented the cake, complete with candles in the shape of '5' and '2'.

For the rest of the evening not a word was said about the school, to Polly's relief. The news would filter out soon enough but she wasn't in the mood to discuss it tonight.

The following day Marjory suggested they put yesterday's news to one side and concentrate on the job in hand in fairness to the pupils.

Polly found that hard. It gnawed at her all morning, knowing she might not get another dream job like this.

It had come just when she needed

it, having packed in her job at the city school where she'd worked since leaving college.

She'd been dating the visiting music teacher off and on for a few years. Though they got on well enough, in Polly's view the relationship was going nowhere.

He wanted them to get married and, eventually running out of patience, went on to marry another teacher in the school after a whirlwind romance.

Polly simply couldn't face continuing working there.

It was Izzy who had alerted her to the vacancy. No-one was more surprised than Polly when she got the job but she took to it immediately, not least because the little school was devoid of some of the social issues in her previous school.

She found working with a smaller number of pupils enjoyable and rewarding. The only downside was that it was part-time work.

Polly had always meant to seek additional employment but, because she somehow managed, she hadn't got round to it. Now she would have to.

She debated with herself as she cycled home over what she could do. It would have to fit in with her mornings at the school. Bar work, for example, wouldn't do because of the late hours.

She was still deep in thought as she parked her bike in the hallway and retrieved her mobile from her backpack.

It was then she discovered she had several missed calls from her mum.

She phoned her back, fervently hoping there was nothing wrong.

She and her dad were due to head off next day on yet another jaunt in their campervan. It was a lifestyle they had warmly embraced since retiring last year.

'Mum, what's up?'

'It's Izzy. She fell and broke her wrist.'

'Oh, that's awful! How did she do it?'

'She tripped over the hose when watering her garden this morning. She phoned me and I dashed round and took her to A&E.

'She's back home with her arm in plaster, in pain and feeling sorry for herself.

It goes without saying that your dad and I will cancel our trip.'

'You'll do no such thing, Mum. I can drop in every day, do things or take her shopping or wherever she needs to go. She's got loads of friends who'll offer to help, too.'

Plans for additional employment would have to be put on hold. Polly couldn't imagine her independent aunt taking too kindly to being so indisposed, though.

'We'd planned to be away for two weeks,' Fiona protested.

'You should go,' Polly repeated. 'I only work mornings. I can go to Izzy's from work every day. Make lunch for us both and spend some time with her.'

'If you're sure . . .'

'I'm very sure. Now, go and get packed. I'm going round there now.'

'All right. I'll come by later with some microwavable meals and treats for her.'

Garden Tour

'I've only broken my wrist — I'm not ill!'

Izzy's feisty response to Polly's sympathies was typical. She sighed.

'Don't think I'm ungrateful for all you've offered to do over the next few weeks, Polly, but do you know the worst bit? Even worse than not being able to cycle?

'It's not being able to use your birthday gift. By the time I'm mobile again many of the flowers will be past it.'

'I'll take you, silly! Any time you'd like to go,' Polly assured her.

The next afternoon she helped an excited Izzy out of the car at Heatherton Hall. Her eyes swivelled to the display of fruit scones in the window of the tearoom as they passed. She hoped there'd be some left when they'd finished, which wouldn't be any time soon.

Izzy hot-footed it into the walled garden, exclaiming with each step and stopping to sniff flowers and stroke foliage.

'Oh, I wonder what that is.' Izzy pointed to a shrub at the back of a deep border. 'It looks familiar.

'Polly, would you be so kind as to tell me what the label says?'

Polly, whose knowledge of plants could be written on a postage stamp, took a step on to the border and lifted the label.

'Hoi, I've just planted things in there!'

Polly almost overbalanced and turned, to see the owner of the irate voice charging up the path towards them.

She stepped back sharply on to the grass under the stern gaze of the young man.

'I'm so sorry but I took great care to step in between the plants. I was only . . .'

'There are signs everywhere asking people not to go in certain areas. You've no idea of the damage we get here.'

His brows were knitted together as his arms gesticulated.

'It's entirely my fault.' Izzy intervened

14

with that soft, persuasive tone Polly knew so well.

Izzy stepped forward and read the name on his badge.

'Steve? You can blame me. My niece brought me as I can't drive at the moment.' She raised her arm in the sling. 'I asked her to read the label on the plant for me.'

Steve opened his mouth to reply but Izzy spread her good arm in a sweeping wave.

'Do you know, Steve, it's years since I've been here and I must say you are a credit to the Hall for keeping the gardens in such splendid condition.'

His face softened.

'It's not just me. There's a whole team of us.'

His hair, which glinted in the sunlight, had the same reddish tinge as his stubble, Polly noticed.

He turned to her, his eyes like two swirls of chocolate locking with hers and giving her a little tingle.

'Just stay off the borders — please.'

He carried on his way.

'Don't worry, we will!' Izzy called to his back.

When he was out of sight she turned to Polly.

'Right, let's get the name of that plant.'

'No fear!'

Izzy reached into her bag for her mobile.

'Take a photo of it on my phone. I've got an app that identifies plants.'

An hour later Polly's head swam with names of plants both Latin and English.

They'd been round the walled garden, the secret garden, the rose terrace, the herbarium and the woodland walk. It was clear that Izzy was loving every minute.

Marjory would be pleased to hear her suggestion had been a hit.

Help Wanted

'Oh, that was wonderful, thank you again! I shall enjoy coming here often.' Izzy linked arms with her niece as they followed the path back to the car park. 'I'm going to steal a few ideas for my own garden.'

'I didn't expect anything less,' Polly replied with a chuckle.

'Now it's my turn to treat you. Let's go for coffee.'

The pile of scones under the glass dome in the café window had diminished but there were still a few left.

They walked through the busy café to the terrace outside the French windows and sat down at one of the wrought-iron tables. Troughs and old sinks filled with alpines and trailing plants bordered the terrace.

There was also a stand with plants for sale.

'What can I get you?' The smiling, pony-tailed young girl retrieved her tablet from the pocket of her apron.

'We'd like an Americano, a skinny latte and two scones with butter and jam, please,' Izzy told her.

The waitress tapped the screen a few times and assured them she'd be right back with their order.

'I suppose you'll be signed off work,' Polly guessed.

'I'm not, actually. I phoned in to tell my boss what had happened and said I would take a few days of self-certified sick leave at first.

'The good thing about working from home is I can work when it suits me. I plan on doing a couple of hours at a time.'

Izzy worked as an accountant.

'Will you manage to do work with those spreadsheets using one hand?' Polly asked, unable to imagine keeping all those numbers in order.

'I'll be slow, but, yes. Luckily it wasn't my 'good' arm that was broken.'

Trust Izzy to see the positive angle.

'You must let me help you in other

18

ways till Mum and Dad return. After that she'll take over. You know what Mum's like.'

'Tell me about it! As it is I won't need to cook for a week thanks to the amount of food she brought round.

'Your company would be welcome any time you'd like to come round, Polly. My friends are going to drop by, too.'

Their order arrived and the scones tasted just as good as Polly imagined.

As she ate she noticed the waitress seemed to be doing everything herself — serving food, clearing tables and taking orders, all at a fast pace.

Maybe the café wasn't usually this busy, or she normally had help.

When they went to pay at the till she noticed a sign stuck to it.

Part-time Help Wanted.

How part-time? There was no harm in asking.

'What sort of help are you looking for?' she asked the same young girl.

'It's the same as what I do plus looking after the gift shop.'

She indicated an area displaying gifts for sale across the hall.

'I might be interested, depending on the hours,' Polly told her, noticing the look of relief on the girl's face.

'The manager's out just now but if you'd like to give him a ring he'll let you know.

'I hope it works out. I could do with a hand!'

The number was jotted down and handed to Polly.

'Thanks for that. I'll call later.'

After she had dropped Izzy off with her plant purchases Polly went home and phoned the number. She hardly dared to hope the hours would suit her.

'Dennis speaking.' The voice sounded pleasant.

Polly explained why she was ringing and that she worked mornings at the local school.

'I see. Well, the café and shop are open from ten till four every day but the staff continue until five o'clock. Afternoons are our busiest times.

'Do you think you could start at one?'

'Yes, I could.'

Polly didn't finish at the school until 12.30 but it was only a few minutes' cycle ride away, less by car if it was raining.

'Would you be able to work occasional weekends to cover staff holidays?'

It was extra money. Polly said she could.

'Do you have any waitressing experience?'

'I was a waitress in Cavellini's Café in Dalcleish during my teens. It was while working my way through college.'

That seemed to satisfy Dennis who went on to explain conditions. The rate of pay, as Polly had expected, was little more than the minimum wage, but she was in no position to barter.

'If you'd like to come in on Monday I'll give you a week's trial,' Dennis offered.

First Day on the Job

'Nice to have you on board, dear.' The cook's voice was warm and friendly. Polly was impressed at how she could multi-task as she spoke.

'Thank you, Mrs McTavish. It's nice to meet you. It's been a while since I waitressed but I'm sure it'll all come back.'

Polly tied the apron she'd been given around her waist.

Mrs McTavish floured her rolling-pin and flattened what Polly guessed to be scone dough as she spoke. Her grey, wiry hair was threatening to escape the bun at the nape of her neck.

'I hope so because, as Amber will tell you, there's no time to slack here.'

'I'm not afraid of hard work,' Polly assured her.

Mrs McTavish looked over her shoulder for a moment and eyed Polly up and down.

'That's good. I hope you last longer than the other two.'

Polly wondered what she meant but from the manner in which the older woman was stamping out rounds from the dough she guessed it was time to get on with work.

She soon discovered that some people just came for hot drinks and cake. They didn't want necessarily to buy a ticket to walk round the gardens.

Polly could understand why. Mrs McTavish's soup, sandwiches and baking were fresh-made every day. They smelled and looked delicious.

Polly soon got the hang of her job, even using the tablet for orders which was a definite step up from her days with an order pad and pen.

She was glad she'd arrived early enough to find a quiet spot to eat her own sandwich before starting work. She didn't get a chance to sit down all afternoon.

People started to drift away as four o'clock approached. She saw a man cross to the counter and wondered if Amber would serve him or tell him they were just closing.

'Polly?'

'Yes.'

He held out his hand.

'Dennis. We spoke on the phone. I hope your first afternoon has gone well.'

'I think it has. Thank you for giving me the chance.'

He held her hand for a tad longer than Polly would have liked.

'My pleasure.'

He turned away and seemed to scrutinise the display cabinet.

Polly estimated him to be in his late 40s. He was tall and slim and clean-shaven with hair combed forward as if to disguise a receding hairline.

Mrs McTavish came through from the kitchen, wiping her hands on a towel.

'Ah, Mrs McTavish. Seems to have been busy today.' He was now stooping to see the food on the shelves.

'Can't complain, Dennis.'

Polly detected a change in the cook's tone.

'I see there are two scones left. Well,

we can't let them go to waste, can we? It's not as if you can offer them again tomorrow.'

Polly watched as he helped himself to a paper bag from behind the counter into which he put the scones.

Without another word he crossed the hall and went through a door marked 'Private'.

Mrs McTavish returned to the kitchen and Amber picked up a tray and went out on to the terrace, making Polly wonder if she'd dreamed it all.

Polly took Amber's lead and removed the seasoning, sauces and laminated menus from the outside tables. Together they tilted the chairs inwards towards each table.

They did the same with the inside seating area except for tilting the chairs.

Everything had been wiped down and tidied away by quarter to five.

'You did well, dear,' Mrs McTavish pronounced as she bundled dish towels into her bag, presumably to take home to wash.

The deep kitchen sink had been scrubbed, the hob gleamed and bowls and chopping boards were laid out for the next day.

'Thanks, I enjoyed it. I'm looking forward to putting my feet up tonight, though!'

'You can have one of these while you're relaxing.' Mrs McTavish retrieved a cake tin from a cupboard and opened it to reveal half a dozen fruit scones.

She divided them into three paper bags and handed one to Polly and one to Amber.

'Enjoy.'

'I will!'

'She always does that,' Amber remarked when they were outside. 'I'm glad you're working here. Makes my life easier.'

'I'm glad, too.' Polly set off on the bike and headed to Izzy's so they could both enjoy a fresh scone.

Later that week there were rumblings about the school. Mrs McTavish batted the news away.

'I'll believe it when I see it.'
It didn't stop Polly from worrying.

In the Potting Shed

On Friday Polly forgot to check the weather forecast. By mid-morning the sky was gun-metal grey.

Luckily she always kept a packaway jacket in her backpack which kept her clothes dry for the short ride to the Hall, by which time the rain was coming straight down.

She parked at the back of the house as usual but didn't go in. She'd feel obliged to start work and she still had to have lunch.

She looked around for shelter. There were a number of outhouses that all seemed either locked or a bit ramshackle.

As the rain trickled off her hood on to her lunchbox she spotted one open door and made a run for it. There was a sign above the door. *Potting Shed.*

No-one would mind, surely?

She pulled down her hood and had a look around. There were benches along one wall with a collection of terracotta pots in different sizes. Underneath were bags of compost. An old armchair sat in the middle of the shed.

There was a pot with plant name tabs and a couple of pencils that looked like they'd been sharpened by a pen-knife. The place smelled of damp soil.

Polly sat down on the armchair and bit into her sandwich, scanning the walls with its maps and plans of the gardens and old photos of grim-faced gardeners. She wondered how many gardeners had come through this bothy.

She stiffened as she heard someone run across the cobbles then appear in the doorway, giving her no time to make herself scarce. It was Steve.

She looked up and jumped to her feet.

'I'm sorry.'

He held up his hands.

'It's fine. Please finish your lunch.'

'I seem to make a habit of this.'

He looked puzzled.

'It was me who walked on your flower border last week.'

A spark of recognition crossed his face

accompanied by a flicker of a smile.

'Ah, yes. The cycle helmet fooled me. Back so soon?'

He leaned against the potting bench and folded his arms, his hair plastered against his head from the rain.

'That same day I got a job in the café here. I also work at the village school, though, so I only have half an hour to get here and wolf down some lunch.'

She looked at her phone screen.

'I need to get going. Thanks very much for letting me stay.'

'Any time,' Steve said as she made a dash to the house.

She was sure his eyes were boring into her back.

★ ★ ★

All weekend Polly thought about Steve. She couldn't get the image of him out of her mind. There was something about the way the rain had rearranged his hair and highlighted his eyelashes that she found attractive.

He was also a much calmer version of the person she had met the week before. Maybe they had caught him on a bad day.

She had offered to take Izzy to the gardens again on her days off, in the hope of seeing him, but the rain didn't let up and Izzy didn't fancy trudging about in wellington boots whilst balancing an umbrella in her one good hand.

Instead they went to the cinema and got a Chinese takeaway afterwards to take home.

'Is there anything I can do for you while I'm here?' Polly asked when they'd eaten and she'd cleared away the food containers.

She was bushed, having spent the past week juggling two part-time jobs with lots of cycling in between.

'Since you ask . . .'

Polly spent the next couple of hours doing household chores that Izzy couldn't manage just now.

She was happy to help and, in any case, her mum would take over the following weekend when she got home.

Her eyelids were growing heavy by the time she got home and started looking out her own things in readiness for the week ahead. When her head hit the pillow at nine o'clock she was out like a light.

Over breakfast she checked the long-range forecast. It was due to be mainly dry this week except for the odd shower.

That was good news as it meant she could cycle most days. It was great that she now had a financial cushion from working at the café but she didn't want to use her car without good reason.

Fortunately her mortgage was small, thanks to her parents giving her a chunk of money when she left college to put down a deposit on a place of her own.

Her little terraced house was a steal and, luckily for her, the previous owner had installed decking and artificial grass in the back garden so it was maintenance free.

Devious Dennis

It was Wednesday before Polly saw Steve again. One of her charges was off school with a tummy bug so Marjory, who was aware of Polly's lunchtime rush at the café, told her she could leave early.

It was a sunny day so she plonked herself down on a bench in a corner of the walled garden beside a water feature.

Bees were working the flowers dripping from a nearby pergola and butterflies flitted around a buddleia.

A smattering of people were strolling from border to border while another gardener was on his knees, weeding.

The tranquil scene gave Polly a sense of what it must be like to work with nature. Although she couldn't tell a plant from a weed the beauty and the feeling of calm it instilled was impossible to ignore.

'Hello again.'

With a flutter in her chest she squinted into the sun to see the silhouette of Steve.

He sat down beside her, a broad smile

on his face.

'You have the best job in the world, do you know that?' she remarked.

Steve rolled his eyes.

'On days like this I would agree, but sometimes I could see it far enough.'

She could tell that his comment was tongue-in-cheek and that he really did enjoy his job.

'Have you been working here for a long time?'

'Nearly a year.'

He picked bits of dirt off his hands as he spoke.

'Where did you work before that?'

'Ah, well, that's a bit of a story . . .'

Steve scratched his head, as if wondering where to start, then suddenly jumped to his feet.

Polly looked in the opposite direction and saw Dennis approaching. His face was dead pan.

'Shouldn't you two be working?' He looked at them both.

'It's not quite one o'clock yet,' Polly replied, stuffing her lunchbox into her bag. 'Steve was just making the newbie feel welcome.'

Which is more than you have done, she added silently.

All Dennis ever seemed to do was snoop around. He never missed the end-of-day, left-over food, though!

She slipped quickly out of the walled garden through the archway in the yew hedge but could still hear Dennis berating Steve.

Polly felt bad for getting him into trouble. She would make a point of apologising to him next time she saw him.

When Dennis appeared in the café as it was closing he made no comment about their earlier interaction.

It was on the tip of her tongue to defend Steve but just then Mrs McTavish came through from the kitchen and spread her arms wide.

'You're out of luck today, Dennis. We've sold out.'

It was an Oscar-winning performance by Mrs McTavish who, Polly knew, had secreted some lemon drizzle cake for all of them.

Dennis let out a deep sigh and flounced off like a petulant child.

'What does he actually do here?' Polly asked the older woman.

She'd been itching to know since she arrived and felt she knew Mrs McTavish well enough by now to ask, especially since it was obvious he was not a friend.

Amber had departed sharply as she had a dental appointment. The two women were on their own.

'Good question,' Mrs McTavish scoffed, unwrapping her apron from her ample girth and reaching for her coat. 'I've wondered the same thing myself ever since he came here.'

'How long ago was that?'

'It's only been about eighteen months. It just seems longer!'

She looked around the hall and up the central stairwell, then over her shoulder.

'Put your coat on. We'll walk down the drive together. Sometimes I think these walls have ears.'

Polly walked beside her bike and carried Mrs McTavish's bag in the basket on the front. When they were clear of the building the story started to emerge.

'It was wonderful being employed here before Dennis came. The Aitkens were a joy to work for.'

'Who were they?'

'The owners. They're still here, it's just you don't see them often.'

'What do you mean they're here? They're in the house?'

'They occupy the top floor. Patricia, or Pat as she's called, had boundless energy. Well, they both had and they ran the place efficiently and made everything seem like fun.

'She was very arty and ran all sorts of classes in the outbuildings.'

That must have been what Izzy was talking about.

'What happened?'

'Pat's rheumatoid arthritis, which had been dormant for years, flared up suddenly and she had to stop doing everything.

'Dear Richard switched all his energy into looking after her.'

'Oh, that's so sad! I don't think I've seen them.'

'They go out at weekends but during the week they don't venture out often. They have a balcony so they can see their beloved gardens and things going on.'

'Where does Dennis come into it?'

'As far as I know he's the son of friends of friends who recommended him as the Aitkens needed someone quickly to manage the place.

'It was a bad choice, is all I'll say.'

Polly nodded.

'He had a go at Steve, the gardener, today. It was quite uncalled for.'

'Yes, Dennis is a bully for sure. Poor Steve. A troubled young man. Nice, but troubled.'

Steve's Story

What had Mrs McTavish meant by 'troubled'? Polly owed Steve an apology anyway so next day she sought him out when she arrived.

She spotted him as she rounded the corner of the house. He was scything in the woodland area.

Polly padlocked her bike and waded through the wildflower meadow towards him, mesmerised by the rhythmic movement of the activity and swish of the blade as it sliced through the long grass.

When he saw her his face broke into a broad smile and he laid down the scythe.

'Hi, Steve, don't let me disturb you. I just wanted to say I'm sorry that I was the cause of Dennis going on at you yesterday. I felt like I abandoned you.'

He waved away her concern.

'Don't worry about it. It wasn't personal. Dennis doesn't like anybody.'

'I'm coming round to thinking the same. I know Mrs McTavish isn't a fan.'

Steve made no comment, just wiped his forehead with his sleeve and bent down to pick up his bottle of water.

'I bet you haven't had your lunch, have you?' He glugged some water.

'Not yet,' Polly said.

She didn't mind as she could eat her banana on the way to the house.

'Here, sit on this.'

He untied his green fleece from around his waist and laid it at the foot of a large oak.

'You'll be out of sight of the house.'

'Thanks.'

Polly was eager to prolong the conversation with this attractive man. She lowered herself to the ground and stretched her legs out in front of her.

'Yesterday you started to tell me about your employment before here.' She peeled the lid off her yoghurt carton and scooped up a spoonful.

Steve, sitting cross-legged on the grass a short distance away, looked directly at her.

'I'll give you the potted version. I was

40

a gardener after leaving agricultural college. I started going out with a girl who became my fiancée, then my wife.'

He was married? Polly knew a pang of disappointment.

'We lived in rented property and were saving to buy a house. We wanted somewhere with a decent garden for our daughter to play in.'

He had a daughter, then.

'Gardeners aren't well paid and neither are shop assistants, which is what she was. We faced a long wait before we'd be able to gather a deposit together.'

Polly listened but said nothing, unable to guess what was coming.

'When this person we knew vaguely introduced us to a get-rich-quick scheme it seemed like the answer . . .' His voice trailed off.

'But it wasn't,' Polly finished for him.

'Well, I gave up my gardening job and put all my energy into the scheme, believing the money would flow in. It was OK at first but, long story short, we lost all our savings.'

Polly gasped.

'That's awful! You must have been devastated . . . and angry!'

Steve nodded sadly.

'It was the worst time of my life. My marriage didn't survive the fall-out. My wife — or should I say, ex-wife — went to live with her parents and I got a job here.

'Fortunately Groom's Cottage was vacant and I was allowed to rent it, otherwise I don't know what I'd have done.'

'I'm so sorry. I don't know what to say. Do you see your daughter?'

He nodded and his smile returned.

'Yes. She comes to stay every other weekend and we FaceTime in between. There's no problem with access. We agreed between us what would work best for everyone.

'The main consideration was Freya and I'm pleased to say she seems remarkably unfazed by it all.'

Judging by the loving way he spoke about her Polly knew he'd be a good dad.

'Freya. What a charming name. How

old is she?'

'She's six.'

'I'm sure she's adorable.'

Especially if she looked like her dad, Polly added silently.

Steve stood up, retrieved the scythe and leaned on one of the handles.

'Er, I was wondering, do you want to meet for a coffee some time? We always seem to have these snatched conversations and, well, it's nice talk to someone. That's if you want to.'

Polly got the impression that, deep down, he was lonely.

'I'd like that.'

★ ★ ★

Polly floated around the café that afternoon, thoughts of meeting Steve giving her a shiver of excitement.

She was in such a dreamy state she earned herself a raised eyebrow from Mrs McTavish more than once.

She hadn't been out with anyone since she'd pulled the plug on her last relationship and moved jobs.

It had been liberating not to have to think of anyone but herself but there was a lot of day to fill since she had been working only part-time.

Izzy encouraged her to go on long cycle rides around the countryside, with her or on her own. She visited her parents and invariably got inveigled into helping with some chore or other.

She met friends for coffee or to go for a walk but was fortunate in that she actually enjoyed her own company. Occasionally she indulged in bingeing on box-sets or read a book from cover to cover in one go.

Meeting Steve had somehow made her feel alive again, however.

At the end of her shift, when she was handed her goody bag containing a piece of millionaire's shortbread, she chided herself for getting carried away.

Steve hadn't said it was a date. It was coffee, for goodness' sake. Almost certainly she was overthinking it.

On Friday evening she took Izzy for

a food shop and picked up a few basics, including bread and milk which they took to her parents' house. The couple were due back the next day.

'I'm bracing myself for your mum coming round on Sunday, no doubt armed with more food parcels,' Izzy said. 'I plan to ask her to come early and get her to take me to the gardens at the Hall.

'Do you want to come with us or do you see enough of the place during the week?'

Polly was quite relieved her mum was coming home. She loved Izzy but she had visited regularly over the past two weeks and was frankly exhausted.

'I'll give it a miss, if you don't mind. I'm sure you and Mum will have lots to catch up on. In any case I'm meeting up with a friend for coffee.'

Izzy didn't need to know it was Steve.

'That'll be nice for you. There's nothing like a good chin-wag between friends, is there?'

'Nope. Now, is there anything I can do for you before I head home?'

She planned a lazy evening with her feet up, watching TV. It had been a long day.

Izzy considered.

'Since you ask . . .'

Walk and Talk

Polly felt like a teenager again as she waited for Steve to arrive. She didn't have to rush about the house tidying up and cleaning because she kept on top of everything anyway.

She felt he'd be appalled, though, if he saw her back garden with all its fakery. Fortunately her front door opened up directly on to the pavement so there was no front garden to be ashamed of.

They had agreed to head in the opposite direction to Heatherton village and the Hall, to avoid bumping into any school pupils or regulars at the gardens. Not least Izzy, along with her mum today, neither of whom would miss the opportunity to say something embarrassing.

A car drew up in front of her house and a few moments later there was a knock at the door. Her heart skipped a beat when she opened it and saw Steve, dressed in jeans and a polo shirt.

She could see the comb marks in his

hair. He certainly scrubbed up well!

'Hi, come on in. I'll just get my bag and a jacket.'

She tried to sound casual but was sure her legs were shaking.

He followed her inside and she could see him appraise the little sitting-room as she scooped up her bag.

'You have a very nice house.' He nodded in appreciation.

'Thank you. It's very small but it was all I could afford even with the help of the Bank of Mum and Dad. Ah, I see you're wearing comfy footwear.'

He flexed his toes inside his trainers, a look of amusement on his face.

'Your point being?'

'I just thought, since it's a nice day, I could show you a glen not far from here where there are some nice walks.

'A little further on there's a place called the Coffee Shack with outside seating and superb views over the glen.'

She thought it would be less awkward if they strolled in the fresh air rather than stare at each other across a table.

Steve seemed almost relieved at the suggestion.

'That sounds like an excellent plan.'

Outside, she couldn't fail to notice his car was even older than hers. It had a couple of bashes and one of the wheel arches had tape on it.

She made no comment but got in the passenger side, noticing as she did so a glittery pink tiara on the back seat.

Polly gave directions and soon they were pulling into a woodland parking area.

They checked out the information board showing several colour-coded walks of varying lengths.

'How energetic do you feel?' Polly figured Steve could probably do them all with very little effort.

'I'd be happy to do the red one. It's the longest but looks like the most interesting route and it's only five miles. Is that OK with you?'

'I was hoping you'd choose that one. It's my favourite.'

'Ah, so you've done them all? You'll

know all the things of interest to point out, then. Lead on.'

They set off along the path side by side, chatting amiably. Whenever it narrowed or they passed other walkers they had to adopt single file but that wasn't often.

Steve named many of the plants and trees they passed. He spoke about some of their characteristics, too, in a way Polly found interesting. Even so, she hoped he wasn't going to test her later!

After a while he must have realised what he was doing.

'Sorry, it's a gardener thing. I can't help it.'

'It's fine. My aunt does the same. She's the one who was with me that day.'

Steve put his hands over his face and groaned.

'I'd rather forget that day. I was totally out of order and very rude.'

'You had your job to do.'

True, he had been rude, but at least he was sorry for it.

'I had just had a run in with Dennis

50

and wasn't in the best of moods,' he explained.

'That man certainly seems to have a chip on his shoulder.'

'Well, he keeps telling us gardeners how to do our jobs.'

'Is he qualified to do that?'

'No! He doesn't like us using too much of anything, be it compost, feed or weedkiller.

'Just before I saw you he had accused me of planting things too close together. He said it was wasteful.

'I didn't spend several years at college, learning all I know, just to be told how to do my job by someone with no qualifications or experience.'

'You're sounding annoyed again,' Polly said and touched his arm.

He stopped walking, turned to her and threw his arms wide.

'I know, listen to me. Sorry — again! Let's change the subject.'

'Let's not. I'd like you to continue telling me about the different plants.

'I have to confess to knowing little or

nothing about plant life. The way you tell it, like a story, is so interesting.'

As a result of her inquisitiveness the walk took far longer than it should have. Still, Polly enjoyed every minute of it and she felt that all her newly acquired knowledge would help her see her countryside walks in a new light in future.

She found Steve easy company and recognised they were both in a similar hiatus of their lives.

'That hits the spot,' Steve said after sipping his hot drink.

They were sitting on the decking outside the Coffee Shack enjoying a mug of freshly brewed coffee and a scone.

The scones weren't up to Mrs McTavish's standards but were still tasty and they were both parched and peckish after their three-hour walk.

'Mm, doesn't it just,' she agreed. 'I like coming here because it's so remote and who wouldn't want to see that view?'

'I know.' Steve spread jam on his scone top and bit into it.

'Do you like working at the Hall

— apart from Dennis, that is?'

After a pause, during which Steve stared into the middle distance, he spoke.

'I feel . . . safe there.'

Suddenly Polly felt she was treading on eggshells. She'd been making small talk, hoping to learn a bit more about the workings of the Hall.

'In what way?'

'I get on with my job and go home every night. I jog along fine with my colleagues and try to stay out of Dennis's way.

'I like the vastness of the grounds, and the variety of the work.'

Polly didn't want to pry but guessed he'd been badly dented by the experience that resulted in him being at the Hall. She'd try to change the subject.

'Oh, and I also like that Mrs McTavish often leaves a parcel of home-baking on my kitchen table whilst I'm at work.'

He popped the last piece of scone into his mouth and looked over his shoulder.

'I have to say these scones aren't a patch on hers!'

Cheap Tat for Sale

It had been so long since Polly had had a first date — if this could be termed such — that she had no idea what the protocol should be when it came to the parting of the ways.

They had spent much longer than she imagined they would at the Coffee Shack but in truth it had been so relaxing she felt she could have sat there until the sun went down.

By the time Steve dropped her off at home she wondered if she ought to invite him in for food. She was ravenous so guessed he must be, too.

After all, she would be cooking for herself so why not for two?

That would prolong their time together probably by another couple of hours, however. For all she knew he might be itching to get away but was too polite to say so.

The decision was taken out of her hands when he drew up outside her house and his phone pinged.

He looked at the screen.

'I've got my usual Sunday FaceTime with Freya in twenty minutes so I'd better go. I don't want to be late.'

Polly pulled the handle to open the car door.

'Yes, that would be unforgiveable. Thanks again for a lovely afternoon.'

'No, thank you for introducing me to new territory, Polly. I really enjoyed that walk and your company.'

His face broke into a wide smile as he leaned over and kissed Polly on the cheek.

It wasn't totally unexpected as they'd got along well all afternoon but it was validation, she felt, that the attraction wasn't just one-sided.

'See you tomorrow,' he called through the open window as he drove off.

* * *

Polly did indeed see him the next day and over the course of the week their paths crossed a few times.

Usually it was when Polly was on her way to the café for her afternoon's work or when she was leaving.

During some of those encounters they had a quick chat. Once, she saw him when he came to replenish the plant sales stand on the terrace.

She was serving food to customers at the time but they managed to exchange a glance and a smile which didn't go unnoticed by Dennis.

'You two are getting rather close, aren't you?' His accusing voice from behind made her jump.

She was taking advantage of a lull in footfall to have a look at the goods in the gift shop.

These filled her with dismay since much of the display could best be described as tat.

Spinning round, she got the impression he'd been watching her and had been waiting for his moment to pounce.

'I'm pleased to say I get on well with all the other staff members.' Polly surprised even herself with her quick thinking.

She didn't want to make life any more difficult for Steve.

Dennis leaned against a stand which contained boxes of cheap trinkets and flimsy toys, effectively barring her exit.

'Good, good. We're all one big, happy family here,' he said, emphasising the word 'happy' with what looked like a sneer.

He was so close that Polly caught a whiff of his breath. It smelled of stale cigarette smoke.

'That's the order for table ten, Polly,' Mrs McTavish called over from the counter.

'Excuse me, Dennis, I have to go. We can't keep the customers waiting, now, can we?'

She pushed past him and crossed the hall to the café, leaving Dennis muttering under his breath as he walked out on to the terrace.

Polly went over to the counter and faced the cook, hands on hips.

'What was that about? We don't have

a table ten.'

'You looked as though you needed rescuing,' Mrs McTavish explained. 'Mind you, you've already lasted longer here than the last two, I'll give you that.'

'Dennis doesn't bother me.' Polly shrugged.

His type were ten a penny and if he was trying to ingratiate himself with her he could think again.

She fetched a cloth and wiped down the glass on the food-display cabinets and the counter tops. It would save time later and it didn't look like they were going to get a last-minute rush today.

Outside, Amber was wiping tables and sweeping crumbs off the terrace and into the borders.

In the kitchen Mrs McTavish was now almost elbow-deep in flour and butter making a crumble mix so she could make use of the freshly picked rhubarb that Steve had dropped in earlier.

'You know, Mrs T., I don't want to sound snobbish but I'd be ashamed to sell some of that stuff we have in the gift shop.'

'That was Dennis's idea. He poured scorn on all the quality gifts we used to sell, saying he could get them cheaper elsewhere.

'Then he ordered in a whole load of vulgar imports with 'Heatherton Hall' printed on them.'

'Is he actually saving the Hall money with his cutbacks?'

'I don't think anybody knows. He keeps a tight rein on everything.'

'He must be answerable to someone, surely.'

'I think the Aitkens were glad to have someone run the place so Richard could concentrate on looking after Pat.'

'Do you think she'll ever get well again?'

Polly didn't like the idea of the woman being confined to upstairs, especially since she had had such a vibrant life before.

'They hope her condition will improve. The few times I've seen Richard he's told me that she still likes to do art at

59

her own pace. She has friends to visit so they're not short of company.

'They've also taken a couple of long holidays in the sun. I think Richard doesn't want to meddle in running things here.'

'But he'll take control back one day?'

'It's hard to know. They're both getting older so maybe they don't want to be bothered with it all.

'It may have made them realise where their priorities lie. Illness does that to people.'

The following day was 'potted sports day' at school, the first that Polly had ever witnessed. It was very different to 'big' school where lots of pupils took part in a variety of sports.

Because of the smaller numbers in each age group this was more of a team effort rather than individual competition, which Polly found quite endearing.

It was one of a few activities in the run up to the end of the school year. Another was the school outing by bus to Edinburgh Zoo which proved to be a long but enjoyable day.

Finally there was the prize-giving ceremony which was a tear-jerker as it meant saying goodbye to three pupils.

Their departure left a big hole in the school roll, further increasing Polly's anxiety about the school's future.

Extra Work

Mrs McTavish had asked Polly to go to one of the outhouses to get some more cans of soft drinks. It was the coolest place to store them.

This was Polly's first venture into the outer buildings, apart from her brief visit to the potting shed.

Inside it was obvious this had been at one time a hive of industry judging by the paint-daubed tables and chairs on which boxes of supplies for the café were stacked.

Polly could picture it in its heyday, with Mrs Aitken putting would-be artists through their paces. She wondered if this was where Izzy had come for basket-weaving classes.

A sudden noise overhead made her start. She looked up to see a bird flapping about in the eaves and then disappearing through a gaping hole in the roof.

Polly looked around and imagined the sadness the Aitkens must have felt when they had to forgo their activities.

'I thought I'd find you here.'

The sound of Dennis's voice made Polly jump. She spun round and saw his silhouette in the doorway. He seemed to make a habit of cornering her.

'Just replenishing stock.' Polly lifted several trays of cans off the table. 'What with the warmer weather and the school holidays we get through them quickly.'

As she struggled towards the doorway he made no attempt to move nor offer to carry the stock even though it was obvious she was weighed down.

'Would you mind letting me past?'

She wished she hadn't been so ambitious and had made two trips. She would have arms as long as a monkey's at this rate!

Dennis stepped aside and followed her back to the house.

'It's the extra custom I wanted to speak to you about. Do you think you could take on additional hours?'

Polly balanced the bundle on one knee and tried to push down on the door handle with her elbow, astonished that Dennis watched her without offering assistance.

Still, additional hours meant more money, so why not?

'I think I could. What did you have in mind?'

By now she was almost at the café and could see a lengthy queue looking for tables while Amber flitted about as if on wheels.

Mrs McTavish would be champing at the bit.

'The weekends are the busiest. Another two girls come in then but sometimes they're rushed off their feet, especially if it's Amber's day off.'

'Are you asking me to join a rota?'

Polly wasn't sure exactly what he was offering and wished he'd get to the point.

'Well, yes.'

'I'm quite prepared to do it but it would be helpful to know a bit in advance so I can plan my social life.'

Polly didn't have one but that was none of Dennis's business. Still, she would like to know what days she was expected to work.

'I'll draw one up. It's just for the duration of the summer holidays; things will start to settle down after that.

'So, can you work this weekend?'

She was amazed that Dennis seemed oblivious to the mayhem around them from the way his voice drawled and how he jiggled the loose change in his trouser pockets.

'Yes, I can.'

Over Dennis's shoulder she could see Mrs McTavish darting about the kitchen and she felt a pang of conscience.

'Look, I really have to get going.'

'I'll fix the rota to the kitchen wall later.'

Dennis fixed a smile, revealing nicotine-stained teeth, then sloped off to his office.

Polly replenished the drinks stock later and together she and Amber collected some dry baking ingredients from the same outbuilding.

By the end of the afternoon, when

everything had been wiped down, swept up and tidied away, all she wanted to do was put her feet up.

She was grateful that she could go straight home. Now that her mum was more or less taking care of Izzy, Polly had been relieved of the daily visits.

She was going to call in and see her at the weekend to hear all about her afternoon tea at Gleneagles.

First she'd need to find out what hours she'd be working.

The promised rota had failed to appear on the kitchen wall so she crossed the hall past the sweeping staircase to the firmly closed office door and raised her hand to knock.

She could hear him speaking to someone, presumably on the phone, so she waited until it went quiet then knocked again and opened the door.

Dennis jumped to his feet when he saw her as if he'd been caught off guard. He leaned over and closed the lid of his laptop.

'Polly! What can I do for you?'

The office was tastefully appointed with a mahogany desk, floral-covered deep sofa, plush curtains, occasional furniture and family portraits on the walls.

A bit too grand for a manager's office?

'You said you were going to prepare the rota. I wanted to know if I'm working Saturday or Sunday, or both.'

He gave a nervous laugh.

'I was just putting the finishing touches to it. Can you do both days?'

He walked towards her and shooed her out of the room like he was herding sheep.

'Yes, I can.'

'Good, good. See you tomorrow, then.'

Polly shook her head as she collected her bike and began the short cycle home.

She reflected that, whatever Dennis was paid, it was too much! He didn't seem to do anything but hang about the place telling people how to do their jobs.

She'd only been working there a few weeks, though. Maybe she'd get a chance to find out more about him over the course of the summer.

She was grateful for the weekend work, certainly. It would help her to stop thinking about Steve who, she knew, would have a wonderful time with his daughter.

Meeting Freya

If Polly had thought the café was busy during the week she got a shock at how much busier it was at weekends. There was never a lull in proceedings.

As well as the young girls who came in to help wait on tables a young lad was employed to keep the dishwasher stacked and emptied and to assist Mrs McTavish.

Polly learned that lady worked the whole summer season without a holiday. She would take an occasional day off when things were quiet and someone else was brought in to cover for her.

The clientèle was different at the weekend, too, Polly saw. During the week custom was mostly made up of retired couples, keen gardeners or friends meeting for coffee and a chat.

At weekends there were generations of families, day-trippers and often bus tours.

By Sunday Polly was looking forward

to going to Izzy's for a meal after work. Apart from enjoying her aunt's excellent company it would save her cooking.

Today she had indulged herself by driving instead of cycling. She'd worked seven days in a row and felt she deserved a small treat.

Besides, it wasn't as if she wasn't getting enough exercise!

After they'd closed the café door at four o'clock Polly and the young lad were dispatched to the outhouse to collect more stock for the following day.

She was grateful for the company. She'd felt disconcerted last time, when Dennis had paid a visit. Come to think of it she hadn't seen him all weekend.

Maybe he only worked weekdays.

It took several trips to fetch all that was needed. Polly was closing the outbuilding when she heard a car engine and voices coming from the other side of the house.

She wondered if it was the Aitkens returning from a day trip, curious to know what they looked like. She crept along the back of the house till she reached the corner, then peered round.

Instead of the Aitkens' car it was Steve's she saw, parked in front of his cottage.

The car engine was running and one of the back doors was open. She could hear laughter from the house then a young girl ran out, shrieking and giggling, her dark hair flying behind her. She was wearing shorts, a T-shirt and pink trainers.

Immediately behind her was Steve chasing her. He looked happy and relaxed.

He must have sensed he was being watched for he turned his head.

'Polly! I didn't know you worked weekends.'

He crossed to where she stood whilst stretching an arm out to his daughter.

'School's closed for summer so Dennis offered me some extra hours,' Polly explained.

The little girl skipped straight into her dad's embrace.

'I'm sure the money will come in

handy, especially with the uncertainty over the school's future.' Steve scooped up Freya.

'It really will,' Polly agreed, 'though I'm hoping the school will be saved.'

'I hope so, too. In case you hadn't guessed this is my daughter. Freya, say hello to Daddy's friend, Polly.'

It was nice to hear herself referred to as his friend and not work colleague.

'Hi, Polly.' Freya fixed her a stare with the same gorgeous eyes as Steve's.

'It's really nice to meet you. Have you had a fun day with Daddy?'

'I've been here for two nights,' she stated. 'We went swimming today and we went to the play park.'

'Wow! You've been very busy.'

'And now we have to get you home to Mummy, don't we?' Steve put in.

'But I don't have school tomorrow!'

Freya stuck out her bottom lip out.

'I know, sweetheart, but Mummy will be missing you.'

It was a touching scene and Polly didn't want to intrude any longer.

'It was nice to see you, Polly. Now, I have to get this one home to her mother.'

Steve put Freya back down on to her feet and she jumped into the car. His brows came together.

'Were you looking for someone? You stood at the corner as though you were.'

Polly flushed.

'To be honest when I heard the car engine I thought it was the owners coming back. Being nosy I wanted to know what they look like. I haven't seen them yet.'

Steve chuckled.

'I see. Well, they're a lovely couple. I've come across them a few times. They always pass the time of day and ask how I am.'

'They must have been good to work for.'

'I imagine so. Some of the other gardeners talk about those days. Mr Aitken was very hands on and helped out with big jobs, like cleaning out the pond at the end of the season or mending broken fencing.'

'I can't imagine Dennis doing that!'

'Me, neither.' Steve shook his head.

'Daddy!'

'I'd better go. See you tomorrow?'

Polly felt her insides flutter but tried to sound casual.

'Sure. See you tomorrow.'

As Steve's car pulled away she wondered what they would chat about as they journeyed. How sad that they had to cram so much into so little time.

True, they spoke every day but it wouldn't be the same.

On the way down the drive Polly passed a 4x4 with an elderly couple inside. She guessed they were the Aitkens.

They were going slowly enough for her to see they were laughing. Was it something they'd seen or had one of them said something funny to the other?

They looked like any contented couple enjoying each other's company. A bit like her mum and dad.

It was such a shame for Freya that her parents didn't have that. She felt for

Steve, having to be alone until the next time she came to stay.

She'd make a point of suggesting they meet up again for coffee.

Family Meal

'Can't I help, Izzy?' On her arrival Polly had been ordered to sit on the stool at the other side of the breakfast bar on account of looking exhausted, apparently.

Her aunt assured her everything was under control but it was painful watching her operate with one hand whilst she prepared the food.

Although Polly was relieved to be off her feet, her aunt's discomfort was clearly greater.

Izzy sighed in frustration and set down the oven gloves.

'Would you be a dear and lift the quiche out of the oven for me?'

Polly retrieved the heavenly creation and set it down on the dining-table. Typically of Izzy the table was set in perfect symmetry with table mats, napkins and glasses. Polly wondered how long it had taken to do.

'It smells and looks wonderful, Izzy!

Anything else I can do?'

Her aunt nodded towards the fridge.

'The salad's prepared so if you could put that on the table, with the dressings you'll find in the top compartment of the door, that would be great.

'The baked potatoes are ready. All we need now is your mum and dad.' She looked at the clock on the wall.

On cue the door opened and Fiona and Jim breezed in.

'Sorry, are we late?'

'Right on time,' Izzy assured them. 'I hope you're hungry.'

'Starving!' Jim rubbed his flat stomach.

'You're always starving.' Fiona gave Jim a playful push then set down a heavy bag on the floor.

'Here's some produce from our garden, Izzy. We've got a glut of everything at the moment.'

'Wonderful, thank you.'

Polly could detect a mild look of alarm on Izzy's face. She would make a point of offering her help later in preparing the produce for the fridge, freezer or jampot.

They all sat down and tucked in. Polly was ravenous and the quiche was delicious.

'How's the physio going?' Fiona asked.

'Slow and painful.' Izzy groaned. 'I'd thought, when they took the plaster off, I'd have full use of my hand again but it's pretty useless at the moment.'

'Patience never was your strong point, was it?' her sister said kindly.

'Very true. It bothers me, though, that the garden's becoming overgrown. I don't like it looking that way.

'That makes me sound ungrateful, doesn't it? I'm lucky that you come over to cut the grass, Jim. I feel guilty as you've a big garden of your own to look after.'

'I don't mind,' Jim assured her as he helped himself to seconds.

'I know you don't, but I do. Besides, you both took retirement so you could take off when the mood took you.'

'Family comes first. You'd do the same for us if the shoe was on the other foot.'

'Of course I would,' she acknowledged.

'There you go, then.'

Polly listened to the conversation, an idea forming in her mind.

'Can I make a suggestion?'

Jim set down his cutlery and almost choked on his mouthful of food.

'Please don't tell me you're offering to help Izzy in the garden! She wants to keep her plants, not have them killed off!'

'Dad! That's not funny. No, what I was going to suggest was I could ask S–one of the gardeners at the Hall if they were interested in a few hours' work.

'It would be extra cash for them and help you out of a tight spot.'

Izzy brightened.

'That sounds like a perfect solution. I have a friend who has someone who calls himself a gardener but he's nothing of the sort.

'I'd feel confident with someone from the Hall who knew what they're doing.'

'I'll make enquiries tomorrow and let you know how I get on.'

Mondays were quiet and Polly managed to slip out and into the walled garden unseen by Dennis.

She found Steve deadheading roses, a full trug basket at his feet. She explained the situation as quickly as she could and Steve nodded encouragingly throughout.

'I'd be happy to take a look and suggest where I could help.'

'That's super! She'll be so pleased. Would you like to come along this evening and she can show you round?'

'Yes, that's fine. What time?'

'Come to mine about seven and I'll take you along. She lives near me.'

'Perfect.' He gave a broad smile, picked up his secateurs and continued his task.

When Polly returned to the café she sent a brief message to Izzy to let her know.

Steve arrived promptly at seven.

'We'll walk. It'll just take a few minutes,' Polly suggested.

Once Izzy started talking to him Polly would be but a fly on the wall. This way they'd get a chance to chat.

'It was so nice to meet Freya yesterday. She's delightful.'

They were walking in step, their shoulders occasionally touching.

'Thank you. I think so, too.'

Polly was trying to think of something general to say when Steve went on.

'When I was driving her home she asked if you were my girlfriend.'

Polly laughed self-consciously and waited for him to tell her how he'd responded to Freya's question.

That moment was lost as Izzy was waving frantically with her good arm from where she stood in her front garden.

'Your aunt looks pleased to see us.'

'Pleased to see you. She'll be kissing your feet before you know it.'

'Steve! I wondered if it would be you.' Unconcealed pleasure was written all over Izzy's face.

Steve looked sheepish.

'I'm sorry for being so abrupt that

day,' he said sincerely.

'Oh, that? Think nothing of it.'

Izzy linked arms with Steve and walked him round the garden.

Polly trailed behind, listening to the two enthusiasts talk at length about what needed to be done.

'Let's go round to the back garden,' Izzy decided and turned as if remembering Polly was there.

'Polly, darling, we could have a cuppa while we sit in that suntrap at the top of the garden, couldn't we? Would you mind making it?'

'Sure thing,' she replied, grateful to be spared the usual 'Polly, put the kettle on', a much-loved family saying.

Besides, it was good to have something useful to do.

Inside the house the tray was already set up in the kitchen with three mugs, milk, sugar and slices of fruit cake her mum had brought with her yesterday.

Through the open doorway Polly watched her aunt and Steve in animated discussion as she prepared the hot drinks.

It gave her a warm feeling to know that Izzy was going to feel less stressed by having her garden tended.

If Polly were honest she was also being a bit selfish, knowing this arrangement was going to give her a chance to see Steve more often.

Izzy's Garden

'Your aunt's quite a character,' Steve said as they walked back to Polly's place.

They had stayed longer than Polly had envisaged but it had been enjoyable and there were no awkward moments.

They'd had coffee while the sun sank lower in the sky and they discussed the job in hand. When the subject of hourly rate was broached Polly had loaded the tray and absented herself to the kitchen.

'That's putting it mildly,' Polly said now. 'To be fair, Aunt Izzy's company is a tonic and she has a heart of gold.'

'You're telling me! She's insisted on paying me a very generous rate. My car's MOT is coming up so it'll come in handy.'

Polly, who wasn't exactly flush herself, understood. What with the costs of running a home and, presumably, paying child maintenance for Freya, it must be a struggle on low wages.

She remembered Steve saying it

was safe working at the Hall. Losing everything must have been devastating.

Maybe taking on Izzy's garden would help towards building his confidence.

'Would you like to come in for coffee?' she offered when they reached her house. He turned and looked directly into her eyes. She could tell he wanted to accept.

'Thanks, but do you mind if I don't? I need to be up early — and so do you.'

'I'm glad one of us is the voice of reason,' Polly agreed, laughing.

'I'll see you tomorrow evening, won't I?' It was more a plea than a question. 'I'll be putting in my first shift at your aunt's.'

'Of course. Well, see you tomorrow.'

★   ★   ★

The next evening Polly saw Steve's car go past her house and waited half an hour before going round to Izzy's house, not wishing to seem too eager.

She followed the sound of the lawn-mower to the back garden where she found them both. Steve was creating stripes on the lawn and Izzy was tidying up a border.

When Steve stopped the mower to empty the grass box Polly asked if there was anything she could do to help. She was dressed in old jeans and a checked shirt.

'Keep her away from the plants, whatever you do!' Izzy jested, straightening herself up and arching her back to ease it.

'Your reputation precedes you, it seems.' He winked, making her insides flutter. 'I've got just the job for you. Come.'

Polly followed him to the shed where a range of garden implements hung from hooks along one side.

He picked one that looked like a torture implement and handed it to Polly.

'What am I meant to do with this?' She turned it over in her hand, flummoxed.

'Here, I'll show you.'

He guided her, his hand on her back, to the patio where he dropped down on his knees and drew the tool's blade along the gap between the paving stones. This caused the line of moss magically to curl up and drop on the slab.

'Clever! I can do that, no bother,' Polly enthused, taking the tool and copying what Steve had done.

Half an hour later she was beginning to regret putting so much effort into it and the scraping noise was getting on her nerves.

As she drew the blade across the last crack she felt a shadow fall over her. Steve stood, hands on hips, nodding in approval.

'Great job. Now, if you could sweep up the waste and dispose of it I can give you another job.'

Without waiting for an answer he turned to remove dead vegetation from some shrubs.

'Right. I'll get the sweeping brush then.'

So much for thinking she'd be off the hook so quickly!

She swept the moss curls into a pile

and brushed them on to a shovel which she carried to the garden waste bin.

The patio looked so much better. Polly hoped Steve would forget to set another task and she kept pushing the brush across the slabs in an attempt to look busy.

She needn't have worried. Izzy declared it was coffee time and Polly offered quickly to make it.

When she came out with the tray Steve was still working and Izzy was flexing her hand, a pained expression on her face.

'Is it still very sore?' Polly asked.

'No, just stiff. The physio-terrorist puts me through my paces. Apparently movement will return.

'Of course, if I was still twenty-one it would have done that already.'

'Give it time. Here, have a cuppa.' Polly handed a mug to her.

'Steve, have a break. You've been working non-stop since you got here.'

'That's what you're paying me for,' he called from the far side of the garden where he was creating a good tilth on a border.

'I insist. Come and sit down.' Izzy patted the seat beside her. 'I want to pick your brains about a few things.'

The three of them sat and admired the results of their efforts. Even to Polly's untrained eye the professional touches were evident, such as the sharp edge on the lawn and the thinned-out foliage.

'You do well to look after all this yourself, Izzy. It's a big garden,' Steve remarked.

'I'd go mad if I didn't have it. I like to keep it neat and tidy which is why I'm delighted you agreed to help.'

'It's my pleasure.'

'You know, I've thought for a while about making a few changes. Nothing drastic — a few subtle things to draw the eye.

'The problem is I haven't the foggiest idea so if you've any suggestions fire away!'

Steve bit into a shortbread finger and scanned the garden.

To Polly the garden was faultless

thanks to years of dedicated attention by her aunt.

Steve drank his coffee quickly and stood up.

'I hate to say it but that apple tree has seen better days and it's shading the grass. If it was removed you could put a rock garden in that border, with alpine plants in a variety of colours, and dress it in little bits of slate.

'It would brighten up that corner.'

'Really?' Izzy sounded shocked.

'It's your garden, of course. If you don't want it removed you could do less radical things. Like grouping all those big pots scattered around the garden together on a corner of the patio.

'You could introduce taller ones or, if you can get your hands on one, an old-fashioned chimney. They look great with trailing plants growing out of them.'

Izzy's eyes grew wider with every suggestion. She nodded vigorously.

'Yes, yes, I can picture what you mean. Oh, I'd love one of those chimney-pots but where would I get one? I imagine they're hard to come by.'

Steve shrugged.

'Salvage yards. Reclamation yards. There's one up the coast near Montrose.'

Polly could almost see the cogs turning in Izzy's head.

'I could have a look for you, if you like,' Steve offered.

'Would you? Thank you! I'd pay your fuel costs, naturally.'

'Happy to. It won't be this coming weekend but I could have a scout around next week.'

He turned towards Polly, smiled and raised one eyebrow.

'If you'll come with me?'

Strange Sighting

The following week Polly couldn't get to Izzy's on Thursday evening which was when Steve was next due to work there. It was late opening at her hairdresser and Polly needed a trim desperately.

Since appointments were running over, as usual, she left the salon later than expected and went straight home.

A short while later she saw Steve's car go past after finishing his stint. She gave a wistful sigh. They seemed to be like perpetual passing ships.

She decided that they could make a day of it while they were out looking for Izzy's coveted chimney-pot. Steve didn't have Freya this weekend and he'd told her earlier today how much he was looking forward to a day out with her.

Polly had been emphatic that she could not work on Sunday when the week's rota was drawn up and she wouldn't be drawn further when questioned by Dennis.

Fortune favoured the brave, Polly decided with a grin when she looked out of the kitchen window to see a cloudless sky.

Sunday had arrived and the picnic basket, packed with goodies, was sitting by the door.

She'd also made a big dish of lasagne the day before so that, if the opportunity arose, she could invite Steve in for dinner on their return.

She didn't want him to feel obligated to buy her a meal. His extra cash from Izzy was already spoken for.

Polly's heart fluttered in her chest at the prospect of spending so much time with Steve. She paced back and forth, unable to settle to anything and chiding herself for being so nervous.

At last she spotted his car approaching and gathered her things together. By the time she'd locked the door he was already standing beside her, dressed casually in light-coloured clothes and smelling of pine.

'Beautiful morning, isn't it?'

He almost sang the words. It pleased Polly to see him looking so happy.

'Isn't it just? We're so lucky with the weather. I hope you don't mind but I packed a picnic. We're going to be near a beach and we have to eat at some point.'

'Brilliant idea.'

Steve bent down to pick up the basket. When he straightened up he removed his sunglasses and scrutinised her.

'You know, you suit your hair that length. It frames your face nicely.'

All the other times he'd seen her, whether at work or at Izzy's, her hair had been pulled back into a ponytail. Polly had decided to leave it down today.

'Thank you, that's very kind,' she said, touched that he'd noticed.

Once everything was in the car they were soon motoring towards the coast, the light breeze from the open window flicking her hair.

They chatted easily about the passing countryside.

'I had my FaceTime with Freya this morning,' Steve told her. 'Not because I'll be out all day. Her mum's taking her to the cinema late this afternoon so we couldn't manage our usual time.'

'Lovely. Speaking to Freya must be the highlight of your day.'

He turned towards her, nodded and smiled, then returned his gaze to the road.

'I reckon we should go to the salvage place first,' she said. 'What do you think?'

'Yes, let's do that. It'll take long enough to look round it! I haven't been there in years.'

Polly had never been to this place before and found to her delight that it was like Aladdin's cave. There was so much to look at — furniture, kitchen equipment and every household object you could imagine.

After a half-hour of glorious rummaging Steve reminded her of the reason they were there. Polly followed him outside reluctantly so they could concentrate on their search.

It didn't take long to spot a chimney-pot, wedged between two stone troughs. Close up it was much bigger than Polly had imagined.

'Nicely weathered.' Steve said running his hand down the side. 'A good, traditional, hexagonal shape; not chipped or anything. It would look good on Izzy's patio.'

'It looks heavy,' Polly remarked. 'Should we ask how much it is?'

'Not yet. Let's continue looking. There's sure to be more.'

He was right. By the time they'd covered the entire outdoor area Steve had inspected at least a dozen pots in all shapes, sizes and colours.

They were now back at the first one they'd looked at.

'I hope you won't be annoyed with me but I'm going to enquire about this one.'

'I'm sure you know best though I quite liked the one that looked like a crown at the top.' Polly shrugged.

'I liked it, too, but somehow it wouldn't fit with the other things in Izzy's garden.

'We'd already agreed we'll plant lavender in it and this one will work best for that.'

Polly was aware that her tummy was growling. They'd been here quite a while.

'I'm sure Izzy will be delighted with your choice. I'll continue looking round while you go and barter.'

Steve went off in search of a staff member and Polly strolled past row upon row of weird and wonderful farming implements. The place was becoming busy, possibly because it was such a sunny day.

She did a double-take when she saw the back of someone who seemed familiar.

She pulled her straw hat further down her forehead and walked closer, shielded by a tall man who was going in the same direction.

When she was nearer to him she slipped into the shadow of the building where she had a good view of his profile. Her shoulders tensed. It was indeed Dennis.

He was shaking hands with a man who

was wearing a broad smile.

Polly looked left and right. She didn't want to bump into him, especially as she was with Steve. For some reason Dennis didn't like the two of them talking to each other.

He didn't look her way. He strode off in the opposite direction, swinging his arms. Polly thought it strange he didn't have anything in his hand since it looked like he'd just done a deal.

'You'd have been proud of me.' Steve spoke quietly in her ear, making her jump. 'Sorry, Steve. I was . . . daydreaming.'

'Terrific place, this, isn't it? Well, I did a bit of haggling and I hope Izzy is pleased with the price.'

He leaned on the handle of a rusting sack barrow, a huge grin on his face.

Polly forced a laugh.

'You know my aunt, she'll be pleased. Right, let's get it loaded and then head to the beach. I don't know about you but I'm famished!'

'Me, too. Job done, time to play.'

With a bit of manoeuvring they hoisted

the chimney-pot on to the barrow and rolled it to the car park where someone was kind enough to help Steve get it into the boot of his car.

Polly slipped into the passenger seat and looked all around the car park. There was no sign of Dennis.

Lunan Bay

Polly couldn't get the picture of Dennis in the reclamation yard out of her mind. It could have been innocent, of course — he was entitled to days off like anyone else and was free to spend them in any way he chose.

Still, there was a niggling feeling she just couldn't shake.

'Penny for them?'

'Sorry.' She gave a little laugh and fabricated a reply on the spot. 'I was trying to remember if I'd put the ice blocks in the basket. I know I meant to, just to keep everything cool.

'The heat's getting up and there's nothing worse than warm sandwiches, is there? I brought fresh cream, too.'

'Well, if you did forget it's too late now. In any case, stop worrying. We're both so hungry it won't take us long to demolish everything!'

It was only a short distance to Lunan Bay. Steve parked the car and they carried everything they needed along the board-walk between the gigantic sand dunes and down to the beach.

'Wow, it's busy today.'

Polly scanned the beach in search of a good spot. There were groups of people dotted around and children building sandcastles or paddling in the sea.

'Over here.' Steve led the way and set his things down near one of the sand dunes. 'We should get a bit of shelter from the wind.'

'Perfect.'

Polly took one end of the tartan blanket from Steve and together they set it down on the sand and placed their things on top of it.

She kicked off her shoes and dropped to her knees, glad she had lathered herself in sunscreen this morning.

The sea breeze could be deceptive. It was the sort of day one could get sunburned easily.

'Lunchtime?' Polly lifted the lid of the basket.

Steve gave a low whistle.

'Absolutely. What a feast! And, look, you did remember them.' He pointed to an ice block.

They loaded their plates and ate in companionable silence, captivated by the entertainment happening right in front of them.

There was kite flying; cricket; football and sand art. Dogwalkers, joggers and couples passed along the length of the beach. Everyone was taking advantage of the good weather.

Polly couldn't remember ever having felt this comfortable with her ex.

'Have you had enough savouries? There's strawberries and cream for afters.'

'I saw that and, yes, I'd love some. More apple juice?'

Steve reached for the bottle and poured some for them both.

Polly marvelled at his appetite and wondered where he put it all since he was as thin as a pin. Then she remembered his energetic job.

She placed a punnet of fruit and a

carton of thick cream on the blanket between them.

Steve dipped a strawberry and took a big bite. It seemed to collapse, making juice run down his chin.

He cupped his hand to catch the drips, looking helpless and trying not to laugh.

Polly grabbed a serviette and handed it to him. Their hands brushed which gave her a little tingle.

She wondered if he felt it, too.

'This is ridiculous!' Steve grinned, mopping the red stain on his shirt and spreading it wider.

Polly giggled.

'I should have put in a bib for you.'

'I think you should have,' he agreed.

When they'd had their fill they returned everything to the basket.

Suddenly Steve leaned over and planted a soft kiss on Polly's lips.

'Thank you. That was delicious.'

Butterflies flitted around her insides and she felt a flush rise in her face.

'You're welcome. I'm glad you enjoyed it.'

He jumped to his feet, grabbed Polly's hand and pulled her upright.

'Come on, let's go for a walk.'

Making sure everything was secured on the blanket first Polly walked barefoot beside Steve, their fingers entwined.

They paddled in the shallows, the gentle waves lapping their ankles. Despite the blazing sun the water was freezing.

Polly didn't care. She wished she could bottle these special feelings and hoped the day would never end.

When they'd walked as far as they could they turned around, headlong into a strong wind.

'I don't like the look of that cloud.' Steve pointed. 'We'd best move faster.'

Others had had the same idea. All around them people were bundling up their belongings and making a run for it.

Polly hung on to her hat as she and Steve sprinted back to the car. Only a few hardy souls now remained on the beach.

'Just made it!' Steve laughed as, breathless, they closed the car doors before the first fat spots of rain splattered the windscreen.

The weather couldn't spoil their day. They took the scenic route home through a picturesque, winding glen with pretty hamlets.

It was late afternoon when they pulled up in front of Polly's house by which time the sun had made an appearance.

Without waiting to be invited Steve scooped up the picnic basket and followed Polly inside where he deposited it in the kitchen. Sunshine streamed in the glass panel of the back door.

'You're so lucky to have a west-facing back garden. Can we sit outside?'

He turned the key and opened the door. A wall of heat rushed in.

'Of course. Coffee?' Polly offered, cringing with embarrassment over what Steve might think of her garden, if one could call it that.

'That would be great, thanks.'

She switched on the coffee machine and joined Steve outside. He stood, hands in his pockets, looking around at what probably he thought was a mess.

'I like your table and chairs. Very rustic.'

The tiny, wrought-iron table with mosaic top, with its matching chairs, had been left behind by the previous owners.

They fit nicely at the back door and were handy if she wanted to slip outside for fresh air, grab some sun and read a book.

'Thank you. You've probably gathered by now I'm no gardener!'

'Nobody said you had to be. There are other ways to brighten up a garden if that's what you want.'

'I just don't want to have to remember to water plants, that's all.'

'I was thinking more like stringing fairy lights along the fencing.'

'I hadn't thought of that. I do like the idea,' she admitted.

'You could hang a few mirrors on either side to give the illusion of more space. You get some nice outdoor ones these days with purpose-made frames in all sorts of colours and textures.'

'Let me go get the coffee and you can tell me more. Who would have believed my drab little garden could have a facelift?'

They sat for along time in the sunshine, with Steve making further suggestions which wouldn't cost a fortune.

When it started to get chilly she suggested they went indoors.

'Will you stay for dinner? It's nothing fancy. Just a simple . . .'

'I'd love to.' He leaned over and squeezed her hand. 'I'm having a great day. I don't want it to end yet.'

Steve washed and dried the coffee mugs then set the table while Polly put the lasagne in the oven and prepared a small salad.

When they sat down to eat, half an hour or so later, they still hadn't run out of things to talk about.

They spoke about the school and life in general. Polly learned more about Freya.

They were halfway through their meal when she realised he'd taken a candle from the hearth, lit it and placed it on the table.

Afterwards they settled on the sofa to watch a film with Steve's arm around her like it belonged there.

It felt so natural.

Later he kissed her for a long time on the doorstep before driving off. Polly turned and went into the house which suddenly felt very empty.

Secret Hoard

It was difficult not to rush over and wrap her arms around Steve every time she saw him at the Hall. They'd agreed they would be professional, particularly around Dennis who would possibly make life difficult for them if he thought they were a couple.

Polly knew that was what they were. Before he left her house that evening Steve had said he'd like to start seeing her, if that was what she wanted, too.

Over dinner a lot of his insecurities had bubbled to the surface. He'd explained that, after his divorce, he'd vowed to remain single because he didn't want to experience such hurt again.

That was until he met Polly, he had said, reaching across the table to take her hand.

Having been disillusioned in love she understood the need to take things slowly.

He invited her to his place for dinner

that Wednesday. He served up a delicious one-pot chicken dish containing rice and vegetables.

The cottage was charming, if sparsely furnished. Polly could tell it wouldn't take a lot to heat it in the winter owing to the small windows and thick stone walls.

Most endearing of all was Freya's artwork all around the house which he talked her through when they were cuddled up on the sofa in front of the log burner after dinner.

Polly found herself looking out for him when she was at work and even on her day off during the week. She was now working most weekends.

It was difficult to stop thinking about him. She determined not to go round to Izzy's each time Steve was there, especially now that the chemistry between them might be on her aunt's finely-tuned radar.

Today was especially busy at the gardens and the café was going like a fair. They'd had a full mini-bus from a horticultural society on one of their outings.

After a tour of the gardens the visitors had depleted the café's stock.

'Would you be a dear and get some more things from the store, please?' Mrs McTavish asked, handing Polly a list.

The young lad was emptying the dishwasher and there was a trolley load of dirty crockery and cutlery waiting to go in so Polly couldn't ask for his help.

In the outbuilding she went through the list and piled everything together, knowing it would take several trips and hoping she'd have it completed before Dennis made an appearance.

Since that day at the beach she had wondered if she should have told Steve about spotting him in the reclamation yard.

Now she looked around the building, imagining once again what it must have been like until recently.

It was a shame it had become a dumping ground as well as a store for the café and, presumably, the gift shop.

At one end of the room was a pile of stuff hidden under tarpaulins. For as long as she'd been coming in here she'd wondered what it was.

It had to be the old art easels, Polly decided, giving in to temptation. She lifted one end and came face to face with what looked like a mermaid.

It was gloomy under the covering so it was difficult to make out anything else, but she could make out metal railings and other large objects.

'What do you think you're doing?' Dennis stood in the doorway, his arms folded.

Polly jumped and almost fell backwards over an old wooden bench.

'I, I thought I heard something scurrying and wondered if it could be . . . a rat.' Lying didn't come easily to her.

'Thank you for letting me know. I'll put down some bait.'

Dennis's eyes narrowed and he nodded towards the pile Polly had created.

'I'll help you take that stuff over. Mrs McTavish will wonder what's keeping you.'

'Thanks. I'd appreciate the help.'

Polly scooped up a box and headed for the door, her suspicions deepening.

★ ★ ★

That evening she told Steve about both events. He'd come to her place for a meal. She thought it might become a pattern that they take turns to cook for each other on Wednesdays.

Instead of laughing at her suspicions his brow furrowed.

'Not long after I started working there I noticed that a small stone statue which used to be in the hidden garden had disappeared.

'When I asked one of the other gardeners what had happened to it he said Dennis had had it removed because he thought it looked 'tacky'.'

'Tacky!' Polly cried. 'Yet he doesn't mind offering up shoddy merchandise in the gift shop?'

Steve looked thoughtful.

'Come to think of it a few things got taken away gradually over the months.'

'No-one thought to ask him about it?'

Steve shrugged.

'Not me, anyway. I wasn't in a great place when I arrived at the hall — I was just grateful to have a job. Still am.

'I can't afford to lose it so I keep my head down and stay out of Dennis's way.'

Polly touched his arm.

'I understand. Do you think that's where he's been storing those things?'

'Could be. You'd better be careful, Polly. From what you've told me he doesn't like people snooping around.'

'You're right. I'll leave it be.'

Polly put the film on that they'd selected earlier but she couldn't concentrate on it.

As she nestled into Steve's embrace on the sofa her mind whirled. She was convinced Dennis was helping himself to things in the expansive gardens and, for all she knew, the house. Then he was selling them on.

It would explain why he was at the reclamation yard. To be sure she'd have to have a look at what was hiding under the tarpaulin, for a start.

Even if she did uncover a hoard from the garden gathering evidence of him selling them on would be a different matter.

She'd have to tread cautiously.

'We're Together'

The following day, as luck would have it, Dennis was going to Dalcleish to collect something for Mr Aitken.

The café was quiet so, once she'd watched his car disappear down the drive, Polly stole over to the outbuilding and slipped inside.

When her eyes adjusted to the light she gasped. The tarpaulin and everything that had been underneath wasn't there.

She looked around, half-expecting Dennis to jump out. She went back into the café more convinced than ever that he had something to hide.

When Dennis returned with a big box under his arm and went up the grand central staircase to the Aitkens' living quarters Polly tried to act naturally.

She smiled pleasantly to him as she passed on her way to the terrace with an order.

He appeared again at the end of business, seeming happy to be given what he believed to be the last pancake.

Polly busied herself with tidying up, hoping he wouldn't ask her any questions in case her face gave her away.

'Polly!' Mrs McTavish hissed as the door closed behind him. 'Here, have these.'

Polly took a bag which, when she looked inside, contained six golden pancakes.

'I'd rather feed those to the birds than let greedy Dennis have them!' Mrs McTavish tutted.

Polly smiled.

'Thank you! I'll take them to my aunt's tonight. We'll enjoy them together.'

She knew that if she took them home she might eat them all. Besides, Steve would be there.

She didn't want to go too early otherwise she might be roped in to work! She estimated when they might stop for a break and timed her arrival for then.

When she turned the corner at the end of the street she was surprised to see her parents' car parked outside.

She found them in the back garden with Izzy and Steve.

'Hi, everyone.' Polly held the bag up. 'I've brought goodies.'

'Hello, pet. Lovely to see you.' Her mum gave her a big hug. 'It was a great idea of yours to get help for Izzy in the garden. What a transformation!'

'Hi, Pol,' Jim said, lifting her off her feet. 'What's in the bag?'

'Pancakes, made by the one and only Mrs McTavish.'

'I'll put the kettle on.' Izzy stepped into the house.

Steve was finishing off a border and raised a hand in greeting.

It took a few seconds for Polly to work out why the garden looked lighter. Izzy had consented to the removal of the apple tree.

The little scree he'd created in its place was planted up with young alpines of different-coloured foliage. It looked so much better.

'Do you like it?' Steve was beside her, wiping dirt off his hands.

'I can't believe the difference! Where's the tree?' Polly looked around for signs.

'In my trailer,' her dad said with a laugh. 'That's why we're here. It'll do for the log burner once it's dried out.'

'Well, that's recycling at its best, I suppose.'

Steve took her shoulders and spun her round so she was facing the patio. She spotted the chimney-pot immediately, situated amongst the other pots.

'You were right to choose that one. The one I liked would have looked all wrong.'

'You went together?' Jenny's brows rose and she looked at Jim who shuffled his feet and scratched the back of his neck.

Polly slipped her hand into Steve's and put her head on his shoulder.

'Yes, we're seeing each other. I was going to tell you eventually . . . when I managed to catch you between holidays!'

She also hadn't wanted to tempt fate. It was early days.

'I'm pleased for you, love,' Jenny said.

Was that a look of relief on her face?

Her dad winked and smiled then turned to Steve.

'Talking of us going on holidays, which according to Polly is always, would you be interested in doing a few hours in our garden each time we go away?

'It's mainly cutting the grass. We have several big lawns.'

'I could do that,' Steve said.

'Great! Maybe Polly could bring you over some time so you can see the garden.'

'We could come along this weekend, couldn't we?' Steve looked to Polly.

'You don't have Freya so, yes, we could.'

The words were out before she could stop them.

'Who's Freya?'

Steve explained the situation. Izzy beamed and Fiona demanded photographs which then conjured up stories of Polly when she had been a little girl.

The Aitkens Appear

Next day provided an opportunity that Polly only got because Amber had talked her into swapping their days off. After the lunchtime rush hour Mrs McTavish placed 'Reserved' cards on all the inside tables.

This was a new one on Polly.

'Are we expecting VIPs?'

'We have an art society coming for afternoon tea. They do it every year — have done since Pat ran her art classes. She'll be coming downstairs for it.'

Mrs McTavish looked like she'd had her hair done. This event must be special.

Polly's pulse speeded up at the thought of finally meeting the woman.

'Can I help with anything?'

'I've done all the baking, thank you, though I could do with a hand making the sandwiches.'

Fortunately only a dribble of customers came through the café over the next hour, by which time the food was prepared and the tables laid.

Dennis kept emerging from his office, marching around with no obvious purpose then disappearing again.

When a mini-bus pulled up and a group of people got off, chatting and laughing, Polly guessed it was them.

The elegant man at the front wore a fedora which he removed on entering the house. He scanned the hall with a smile.

'Where is she?'

Polly stepped forward and as instructed by Mrs McTavish, addressed them.

'Mrs Aitken will be here shortly.' She indicated the tables. 'If you'd like to take a seat I'll bring tea and coffee to the tables.'

'Thank you, my dear. You must be new — I never forget a pretty face.'

He looked over her shoulder.

'Belinda! How wonderful to see you again.' He brushed past Polly and kissed a flushed Mrs McTavish on both cheeks.

Belinda?

'I swear you look younger every year. How do you do it?'

'Och, away with you, Anthony.' She gave him a playful pat on the arm.

Was that lipstick she was wearing?

It was rather fun watching this pair tease each other until Mrs McTavish made an announcement.

'Here they are.'

All eyes turned to the right of the staircase, to the lift door.

The elderly couple walked slowly, Pat's arm through Richard's. Anthony rushed towards them and greeted them like the old friends they probably were.

Soon everyone was seated and chatting animatedly. It was clear everyone thought the world of Pat.

Polly slipped pots of tea and coffee on to the tables and made sure the cake stands were never empty.

At one point Dennis walked past, bowing and scraping to the group.

Pat called him over and sang his praises to her friends, declaring how she and Richard could relax knowing everything was being taken care of.

Polly cringed. If only they knew.

Two hours later, after much hugging and promises of meeting again, the visitors got back on the bus.

Polly started to clear the tables with help from Mrs McTavish, whose day had been made when Anthony kissed the back of her hand.

Polly hoped finally to meet the Aitkens but when Dennis bounded out of his office and over to the couple she thought her chance had gone.

'Everything go OK?' he schmoozed, his back to the workers as if they didn't exist.

'Really well.' Richard helped Pat to her feet.

'It was so nice to see everyone again,' Pat said with a wistful look. 'Oh, I miss the art world.'

Richard patted the back of her hand.

'You'll be back in it again before you know, darling. You're getting better by the day!'

Did Polly imagine it or had Dennis

jerked upright?

'Now I want to meet the young lady who looked after us so well this afternoon.'

Dennis stepped back and, through gritted teeth, introduced Polly.

'Thank you for all your hard work,' Pat told her with sincerity. 'Why don't you come upstairs so we can have a chat in comfort? That is, if Belinda can spare you.'

'I can help clear these things away,' Dennis chipped in.

Scoop up the goodies, more like!

'That settles it. We'll go up in the lift. See you on the landing, Polly.'

Polly took off her apron and hung it on the back of the door then mounted the stairs.

At the landing she glanced over her shoulder. Dennis was staring at her with a face like thunder and a warning look in his eyes.

Cosy Chat

'How long have you worked in the café?' They were in the vast living-room beside the door which led to the veranda overlooking the garden.

Pat sat in a high-backed chair facing her. Richard told them he'd leave them to chat.

'Since just before the school holidays. I actually work at the school part time as a Support for Learning Assistant. The job here is to supplement my income.'

Pat's brows came together.

'It would be a shame if the school was to close.'

'I know, I'd really miss it. I couldn't believe my luck to have landed such a brilliant job. Did your husband go to school there?'

She saw him more of a public schoolboy.

'No, but I did. Richard's not from these parts.'

'Oh, I . . .' What an assumption to

126

make!

'Don't worry. Everyone thinks the Hall came down Richard's family line, but it was mine.

'We have a distinct lack of males on my side. I inherited from my mother and Richard and I have two daughters. We do, however, have one grandson, so we've broken the chain at last.'

Pat asked about her family and ambitions. She seemed genuinely interested in everything and Polly felt relaxed in her company.

She understood why everyone loved her. At a break in the conversation Polly asked if their daughters lived close by. She liked to think they had some sort of family support.

'Alas, no. We produced two free spirits. One went to live in New York — she's a stage manager in one of the theatres.

'We've been over there many times and have seen some incredible shows with privileged backstage access!'

'Does she come here often?'

'She was last here just after my health

took a downward turn. We do lots of FaceTime calls, though. I think she'll be flying over next year.'

'What about your other daughter?'

'Lives in London. Hazel took after me and became an artist, would you believe?'

Pat raised her hand and indicated the paintings lining the walls.

Polly craned her neck to see better the works around the room. There were landscapes and portraits of people and animals, all beautifully painted.

'Do you mind if I take a closer look?'

'Please do. Are you artistic yourself?'

'I'm afraid I'm not but I do appreciate a good painting.'

For some reason images of Freya's stick people came to mind.

Polly scanned the room. It was sparsely furnished with some fine pieces which she guessed were family heirlooms but which were scratched and dented.

The fabric was threadbare, suggesting this was a happy family home.

She didn't linger on the family photographs as she was meant to be looking at the artwork. One caught her eye.

'I particularly like this one.'

The painting was of the potting shed, cobbled courtyard and the outbuilding Pat had used for her art. It was a good likeness — except the building didn't have a hole in the roof!

'That's one of Hazel's. It's my favourite.'

Polly peered at the signature in the bottom-right corner.

'Oh, I see it now. 'Hazel Aitken'. She has kept her own name, then?'

'She didn't see the point in changing it after she got married — which was good because when she got divorced she didn't have to change it back again.'

Polly nodded.

'I expect you see more of her. London's not far away.'

'She comes up a couple of times a year, yes. Usually for flying visits as she has a busy life in London.

'She lives with her daughter and son-in-law and their three young children. So she has a lot of grannie duties as well as working in her own studio at home.'

'You're a great-grandmother? You don't look old enough!'

Apart from Pat's evident mobility issues she looked no more than sixty-five.

Pat threw her head back and laughed.

'You're very sweet, Polly. I had both my daughters within the first two years of marriage. Hazel was a young mother, too, as was her daughter.

'Another thing that runs in the family.'

Polly didn't want to outstay her welcome as she hoped to be invited again. She returned to her seat and picked up her bag.

'It's been really nice meeting you, Mrs Aitken. I'd best get going.'

'Call me Pat. The pleasure has been all mine, Polly. I do hope you'll pop in again.'

'I will. Thank you again.'

She swept down the staircase and out of the front door, grateful that Dennis didn't intercept her but expecting a grilling tomorrow.

Unexpected

Polly was at work next day when she remembered it was Saturday and that Dennis was usually scarce at weekends. Hopefully he'd have forgotten all about her visit by Monday.

She breathed a sigh of relief and got on with her busy day. She had the evening with Steve to look forward to.

He seemed much more relaxed these days, not the tense person who had barked at her the day they met.

Her feelings for him were growing. Did he feel the same?

He had already eaten when he picked her up at six o'clock. She'd had soup and a sandwich at the café at lunchtime so she wasn't especially hungry.

'Hi, gorgeous.'

Steve leaned over to the passenger side and kissed Polly on the lips, making her insides melt.

'Hi.' She fastened her seatbelt and they set off. 'Just to warn you, my parents' garden really is much bigger than Izzy's.'

'Relax, I'm a gardener. Your dad says he's got a ride-on mower. Those things do all the work.'

'OK. I just don't want you to be under any misapprehension.'

They soon arrived at the house and observed her mum and dad carrying things into the campervan which was parked between the double garage and the house.

'I see what you mean!' Steve's eyes were wide as he took in the expansive garden. 'Why on earth did they want a bigger garden in retirement?'

'They like gardening. As you can see, though, they also like holidaying.'

'Hi, Steve.' Jim strode over and opened the car door. 'Thanks for agreeing to do this. Come on, I'll show you where everything is.'

'No worries, Jim.'

Steve followed him round the side of the house as Polly joined her mum in the campervan.

'Going away again?'

'Not for another week, and then it's only for a long weekend. I'm just replenishing our 'home from home' so we'll be ready to take off. So much easier than packing cases!'

Fiona opened and closed the little cupboard doors as she put everything away.

'Steve's very nice, by the way.'

'I think so, too.'

'Is it serious?'

'Mum! It's much too early to think about that.'

'Oh, I don't know. Your dad and I were engaged within six months. Steve's very different from your ex .. .'

'Thank goodness,' Polly finished for her. 'I do really like him and I like being with him. In fact, I don't like it when I'm not with him.'

'That's an encouraging sign. Come on, let's go and find them.'

The two men were standing beside the ride-on mower. Steve was nodding as Jim pointed things out. Polly could see this was the identical mower to that of the Hall.

'That's settled, then,' Jim said as he acknowledged the approaching ladies. 'Steve's going to take care of the grass on a weekly basis. That way I can forget about it and concentrate on the other stuff.'

'I hope you're paying him well,' Fiona said in a teasing tone.

'I'll pay the same rate that Izzy pays him. Steve can pop along at times to suit him. We don't need to be here — I've shown him where I keep the key to the garage.'

Polly was pleased that he would be earning extra money. It would make things a bit easier.

'I'm glad you've got all that sorted. I know how you fret about the garden when we're away.

'I take it you'll start this coming week?'

'Yes, I'll come along on Tuesday or Friday depending on the weather. As you know I'm at Izzy's on Monday and Thursday evenings.'

He turned to Polly and smiled.

'Polly and I like to keep Wednesdays for us.'

She felt a warm glow inside her at his words.

'Oh, just to say — the following week I won't be able to come as I'm going on holiday with my daughter.'

Polly couldn't remember him mentioning this before.

'It's the last week of the summer holidays,' Steve went on. 'We went away at the same time last year.'

'Are you going anywhere nice?' Fiona asked.

'Yes, to the west coast. My ex-parents-in-law have rented a wooden lodge for a couple of weeks and have invited the three of us.'

The Mermaid

As Steve drove her home Polly felt as if
the bubble she'd created for herself and
Steve had burst. Did this news mean he
and his ex-wife might get back together?

She should never have allowed herself
to fall in love with him. There, she'd said
it.

'I know I've got an appalling memory
but did you mention going on holiday?'
Polly tried to keep her tone light.

'There's nothing wrong with your
memory, I only got the message this
afternoon. Sorry, I should have mentioned it to you first.

'I thought it only fair to tell your parents I couldn't do their garden that week.
Which reminds me, I'll need to tell Izzy,
too.'

'That'll be nice for you all.'

She tried to keep the disappointment
out of her voice.

'Yes, and as it's the last week of the
school holidays I'll see Freya every day.'

And your *ex-wife* . . .

'Thanks to you arranging extra work for me I'll be able to treat her.' Steve pulled up outside her house. 'You're good for me, Polly, you know.'

What did he mean by that? Good as in a source of additional employment?

'I'm glad to hear it. See you on Monday.'

She reached for the door handle but Steve pulled her close and gave her a lingering kiss, making her melt as always.

He pushed a stray lock back off her face.

'Are you sure we can't meet tomorrow?'

'I can't go back on my promise to Izzy to go cycling with her after work. She's desperate now that she can grip the handlebar with her bad hand.

'She wants to do a trial run with me and is convinced the exercise will do her good.'

'I understand.'

Polly went inside and sat staring at the wall, her mind confused.

She'd let Steve get under her skin, and she was sure he had feelings for her, too. But she felt threatened by this turn of events.

She'd seen it many times — couples staying together for the sake of the children. True, they were divorced, but they could just as easily get back together again.

She had no option but to wait and see how things panned out.

Now she couldn't wait until the start of school term so that she'd have a focus. Her job in the café earned her money but working at the school was what she loved.

She saw Steve in passing during the week and he invited her to his cottage on Wednesday. As usual they ate supper and afterwards snuggled up to watch TV.

When she was leaving he held her for a long time. He'd be heading off immediately after work on Friday so she wouldn't see him again until his return.

'I'll miss you.' He toyed with her hair as her head rested against his shoulder.

Polly buried her face into his fleece, trying stop the tears flowing.

'Not too much, I hope,' she managed. 'You ought to have a whale of a time.'

'I will. You can be sure of that!'

* * *

On Friday Polly watched Steve drive off, jealousy tearing at her heart. She spoke to Dennis next day about the work rota.

'I need to go into school a few days next week, before the start of the new term, so I have to go back to working afternoons.'

Dennis considered her for a moment.

'OK. Things are starting to slow down now, anyway. Let's say you finish tomorrow and start again at one o'clock on Monday.'

'Thank you.'

She'd been due to work the weekend but didn't want to argue the point with Dennis.

After she'd eaten that evening she poured a glass of wine and grabbed the slice of Bakewell tart Mrs McTavish had given her.

She sat outside in the evening sunshine. The only sound was of a bee working the honeysuckle in the neighbour's garden.

Polly hadn't been sorry she didn't have plants. She could enjoy those in the gardens either side without it causing her any work!

Looking at her bare plot now, though, she felt dissatisfied about the way it looked. Until Steve had made his suggestions she'd been blissfully ignorant but now she couldn't rid her mind of the visions his artistic descriptions conjured up.

Maybe she could put her weekend to good use. It would help keep those imaginings about Steve's holiday at bay.

Hadn't he said he'd seen some mirrors that would be suitable for her garden at the reclamation yard? She would make that her first port of call on Saturday morning.

★ ★ ★

Excited, she drove up the coast. There would be no picnic today, even though it was a glorious day, for she had work to do.

The place was exceptionally busy and Polly had to sidestep people at every turn to rummage in all corners of the site.

There were dozens of mirrors to choose from. One caught her eye immediately. It was a large oblong with a frame made out of driftwood, giving it a rustic look.

It had a proper rope affixed for hanging it. She was definitely buying that.

A bit further on she found one with a frame made up of fragments of pottery. Some of the pieces had words or patterns on them in different colours. Again she liked the randomness of them and could feel a theme forming.

An hour had passed before she decided she had enough to get started. She'd go to a homeware store for fairy lights.

All she needed was to find someone so she could pay for her purchases. She laid down her choices at the office door and pressed the bell. Shielding her eyes from the sunshine she looked around.

Oh, not again! Dennis was standing not 20 feet from her. Leaving her goods on the ground Polly crept closer.

There was no mistaking it this time. Dennis was being handed money while, sitting in a wheelbarrow between them, was the mermaid Polly had seen under the tarpaulin!

She pulled her phone out of her pocket and took a picture with trembling hands.

Back to School

What should Polly do? She had irrefutable evidence that Dennis was helping himself to things from the Hall.

Or did she? Perhaps he had the blessing of the Aitkens to sell off stuff, or he had things to sell that belonged to him.

What a dilemma.

Pat had told her how fortunate she and Richard were to have someone like Dennis take over the burden of running the place.

If she brought it to their attention and she was wrong, what would they think of her? Steve didn't want to get involved, clearly.

The internal debate went on all weekend until Polly could no longer think straight.

One thing was clear — she'd need more evidence. With no more weekend work and Dennis always hovering in the wings, however, she wasn't sure how she was going to get it.

By Sunday evening her garden had been transformed at very little cost in a way she could never have imagined. She had hung the mirrors opposite each other on the side fences which magically made the little garden seem much bigger.

The circular bird-bath sat directly on the fake lawn, its blue-and-terracotta mosaic tiling contrasting beautifully with the green.

Polly had installed brackets along the back fence from which hung a bird-feeder, several sun-catchers and a windchime she'd made from a box of shells she'd purchased.

Strings of solar-powered fairy lights were looped all the way round the garden. In the dusk it looked romantic and created atmosphere. The best bit of all was that there was no maintenance!

She was delighted with the results and couldn't wait to show Steve. Then, with a jolt, she remembered where he was, and with whom.

These days she paid greater attention to the Hall's veranda and glass doors when she passed to and from work, now knowing where the living-room was situated. On two occasions she exchanged a cheery wave with Pat.

She looked forward to visiting her again but would wait awhile as she didn't want to be a nuisance.

★   ★   ★

On Thursday morning she cycled into the empty school playground, butterflies in her tummy at the thought of the new term and the different challenges ahead.

'Here we are again!' Marjory rubbed her hands together. 'Where did the summer go? I hope you both enjoyed a good break.'

Break? Polly was ready for a holiday. She'd never worked so hard in all her life as she had this summer.

She listened with envy to recounts of her colleagues' holidays: a Caribbean cruise in Marjory's case and two weeks all-inclusive in Ibiza in Clare's.

'Not quite in the same league as you

two but I was lucky enough to get more hours working at the Hall,' she told them. 'It has provided me with a nice financial cushion but it meant I didn't get away.'

Clare gasped.

'Polly, here's me going on about my beach holiday! I'm sorry.'

Marjory also adopted a sympathetic face.

Polly shrugged.

'No, I quite enjoyed it. Besides, if the school is going to close it'll buy me time to find suitable alternative employment.

'Whatever happens I've already decided to take a break in the October holidays.'

Another thing she'd done over the last weekend was to search online for organisations that offered cycling and walking holidays in the UK.

The choice was incredible. One in particular, in the Lake District, had taken her fancy. She knew however that this was partly a knee-jerk reaction to Steve having gone away.

'Let's not assume anything about the

school,' Marjory reminded them. 'Sometimes these things have a remarkable way of resolving themselves.'

'I can't see how,' Clare responded. She looked as though she thought this an incredulous suggestion. 'We've just lost three pupils and next week will gain only one.'

'We owe it to the pupils to give them our full attention. I'm asking you not to dwell on it, that's all.'

Marjory looked from one to the other.

'If there is so much as an inkling that closure is likely I will, of course, join forces with the locals.'

Her face looked determined.

While Marjory and Clare planned out the classes Polly assisted them by printing off teaching materials, photocopying and replacing posters and signage on the walls.

Soon everything was ready for the following Monday.

'Missed You'

With Steve's return imminent Polly found herself checking her phone constantly for messages. Early on Saturday morning it pinged and when she saw his name on the screen her heart skipped a beat.

Morning, gorgeous. Missed you so much. Are you free today by any chance or has Dennis the Menace got you working? X

She let out a breath she'd been holding. He had missed her and wanted to see her.

It didn't sound like he'd got back together with Freya's mum. She'd worried needlessly.

She replied that, yes, she was free. She finished by saying she'd missed him, too.

Come over late morning? I can get a washing done and hung out — got home late last night. I'll make lunch and we can go a walk this afternoon? X

The day became hotter so she took the car to Steve's. Washing was flapping on the line in the breeze and his door was open.

'Cooee!'

'Come through,' he called.

He was washing salad leaves at the kitchen sink. Chopped tomatoes, cucumber and peppers lay on a wooden board.

'Won't be a minute.' He smiled at her.

'Take your time.' She leaned against the door post. 'Good holiday?'

'Great. The weather was brilliant and Freya said it was the 'best holiday ever'.'

He dried his hands and pulled her to him.

'I really missed you.'

'I missed you, too.'

'Why aren't you working today?'

'School starts again on Monday. I told Dennis I had to go back to the hours I did before.'

'Well, it's lucky for me. Come and sit down and tell me what you've been up to.'

She told him about her two days at school and how busy the café had been. She didn't mention the work she'd done in her garden — she'd let him see for himself.

Nor did she tell him of her growing suspicions of Dennis.

'I'm sure your week was more exciting.'

They ate their lunch and Polly listened as Steve spoke about his time with Freya. Her mum, apparently, had only stayed two nights before joining her new partner for the rest of the week on a city-break.

'You have to understand we all get along really well together. Freya's grandparents are history buffs.

'They went off exploring every day, leaving me and Freya to do our own thing, and we all came together in the evening.

'There was a swimming-pool on site plus adventure playground and every day there were activities for the children.

'The week flew by! I was glad to get so much time on my own with Freya.'

Polly felt guilty that she'd harboured such jealous thoughts.

'I'm pleased you had a great time. I really did miss you.'

Steve reached across and took her hand.

'I was hoping you would. I was worried that you might think being with my ex and her parents might change things between you and me.

'I promise it hasn't. In fact, I told them about you. I wanted them to know I was in a relationship.'

His words were like balm to Polly.

'Now,' he added, 'if you've had enough to eat shall we go for that walk? I can show you the rest of the estate.

'It stretches for quite a distance and there's a path at the boundary which leads down to Heatherton village. We could do a loop.'

'Sounds great,' she told him.

Bygone Days

They set out, starting by taking a short-cut through the courtyard. One of Steve's colleagues, who was on a break, called out from inside the potting shed to ask how his holiday went.

Steve stepped inside, followed by Polly who recalled the only other time she'd been in there was when she had been sheltering from the rain and had been found by Steve.

As he chatted to his colleague Penny studied the photographs on the wall of unsmiling gardeners at different eras.

She imagined it must have been uncomfortable to work in woollen trousers and collarless shirts with flat caps on your head. Such a contrast to the light-weight trousers, T-shirts and baseball caps bearing the 'HH' logo that today's staff wore.

In the background were other clues to the era like a car, a perambulator or a maid in cap and apron. It was strange to see the Hall from different angles and the stone steps leading up to the main door which wasn't used any more.

The next photograph showed men cleaning out the pond. They were wearing jackets and the trees in the background were bare. Remembering Mrs McTavish's comment about Richard helping she wondered if he was in the photograph.

If so he was much younger. She'd try to remember to ask Pat next time she saw her.

She was about to move on to the next photograph when her eye was drawn to a water feature at one end of the pond.

It looked like the one she'd seen under the tarpaulin, which she believed was what Dennis had sold at the reclamation yard.

She checked all the other photographs but none were taken at the pond. She'd need to have a look for herself.

'Polly?' Steve was standing in the doorway. 'Shall we go?'

She shook herself out of her reverie

and took his outstretched hand.

She was trying to form the words to ask Steve about the water feature when they turned the corner of the building and bumped into Dennis.

She hadn't expected to see him since this was the weekend.

He viewed them with narrowed eyes.

'Well, well. Can't keep away from the place, can you?'

'Steve lives here,' Polly pointed out.

'I stand corrected. So he does.' With a smirk he marched off.

Annoyed that Dennis had caught them holding hands Polly forgot all about the water feature. Steve seemed unconcerned and led her at a leisurely pace past areas of the grounds she was familiar with.

They went into a woodland with big trees which Steve explained were mature oaks, beech and ash. Above and around them the wind sighed and the leaves rustled in an almost tuneful way, making her forget about everything and soak up the peacefulness.

Steve talked more about his holiday.

'Maybe you could spend some time with me and Freya next time I have her.'

'I'd like that.'

Polly meant it. She looked forward to getting to know the little girl better.

They emerged from the trees and picked up a path that wound round the outside of the woodland. They'd been walking gradually uphill and could see the Hall peeping above the trees to their left.

Below them lay Heatherton village. They ambled downhill between dry-stone dykes until the path stopped at the far end of the village.

Polly had driven through many times but had never had a reason to walk the length of it until today. The main street was lined with cottages and houses in a variety of simple styles, built in the same grey coloured stone as the lodge and Hall.

She spotted that each cottage bore a crest above the door of a crescent moon and stars with 'HH' intertwined in the middle.

It was obvious these had been workers' cottages for the Hall. Perhaps some of the gardeners she had seen in the photographs still lived in them.

'What a charming place.' Polly said. 'It was clever of you to know about that path.'

'I've had plenty of time to get to know all the routes around here.' Steve smiled at her then returned his gaze to the pretty front gardens they were strolling past.

It must have been awful for him to begin with, Polly considered. Alone and in shock after what had happened to his savings and his marriage.

She could picture him, deep in thought, walking for miles to clear his head and try to make some sense of it. She hoped it had provided some healing for him.

'I'm surprised you didn't know about this route, what with working at the school.'

'I'm ashamed that I didn't. In my defence I work part-time and I only started last year. I'm sure I'd have discovered it eventually.'

A side street led to a couple of rows of houses from where she could hear children's voices.

She looked along it and could see children playing in the street. They stopped what they were doing and waved. One of them shouted her name.

Polly gave them a cheery smile and big wave. Her stomach gave a little twist at the thought that these little lives might change if the school closed.

They reached the school which was locked up and quiet. Next to it the occupants of the lodge were out in their garden. Polly had seen them occasionally but had never spoken to them.

The woman stopped sweeping the path when she saw them.

'Nice day.'

Polly guessed she was in her late seventies. Her husband, who straightened himself up from pulling weeds from a border, looked a bit older. He shuffled along the path towards them.

'It's a beautiful day,' Polly agreed. 'You have a lovely garden.'

'Kind of you to say so. It's getting a bit much for us now. When we moved in here, over fifty years ago, it was perfect for our growing family, wasn't it, Walter?'

'Aye, it was that.' He put his gnarled hand on the railings to steady himself. 'Plenty of room for them to play in the back garden and we had a big plot for growing vegetables.'

'You must have worked at the Hall,' Polly guessed.

'We both did. I was a cleaner and Walter worked on the estate.'

'Jack of all trades,' her husband added.

'We work there, too. That is, I work part-time in the café because I do mornings in the school.'

'I thought your face looked familiar. I've seen you in the playground.'

'I'm one of the gardeners at the Hall,' Steve told them.

'It's a good place to work. It's over twenty years since we retired. It was good of Mr and Mrs Aitken to let us stay on here.

'They pop in sometimes. It's always

lovely to see them.'

'Well, it was nice chatting with you both.'

'Nice chatting with you, too.'

Polly and Steve veered into the Hall drive next to the lodge. They took a detour to the pond at Polly's request. She pretended she wanted to see the water lilies Izzy had raved about after her last visit.

However, her eyes weren't on the water but on the empty plinth at the far end where the mermaid used to be.

Coffee and Buns

On the first day of term the playground din was music to Polly's ears. Some children rushed over to hug her while she secured her bike. It felt good to be wanted.

The sole new pupil knew all the others so there were no first-day nerves to deal with. The only issue was getting the children to settle down to do work. All they wanted to talk about was their holidays.

Working in the café had made an exciting change but it was good to have proper structure to the day again.

Marjory spoke to the children about things happening in the coming year just as if there had been no talk of possible closure. Polly wondered if she was a good actress.

At lunchtime she cycled up the drive to the Hall. Walter waved to her as she passed. She wished she could stop to chat but had only half an hour until she started work.

A few minutes later Pat also waved from where she stood on the balcony.

'Polly, I hoped I might see you. You really must come back for a chat.'

It didn't sound like she was just being polite.

'I could pop over after work.'

'Super. You can tell me all about the first day back at school. I'm sure Richard will be pleased to get respite from my chatter!'

She looked over her shoulder as if to check if he was listening.

Polly laughed.

'I'll see you then. Look forward to it.'

She parked her bike in the usual place and carried her lunch bag into the café.

'Is it all right if I eat my sandwich before I start, Mrs McTavish?'

With the schools back in and holiday season over the café was much quieter.

'Of course, dear. Eat it in here in case You-know-who sees you.' Mrs McTavish rolled her eyes.

The afternoon dragged as it was very quiet. Several times Polly wanted to slip outside to try to locate where Dennis had hidden the mystery goods.

She couldn't risk raising his suspicions. He could terminate her employment and she'd lose every chance of uncovering the truth. She must be clever about it.

She told Mrs McTavish about visiting the Aitkens and at five o'clock was handed a bag containing three iced buns.

'Pat's favourites. Give her my regards and tell her I'll get along to see her soon.'

'I'll do that. Thank you for these.'

'I'm glad you're getting to know her. Maybe she'll get to hear about what Dennis is doing to their place.'

Leaving that thought hanging the older woman walked off.

Mrs McTavish knew more than she was letting on about his misdeeds, that was obvious. How much?

Pat was sitting in the same chair as last time. Richard made them both coffee.

'I'll have mine in the other room and leave you ladies to chat,' he said with well-rehearsed diplomacy.

'See what I mean?' Pat said when he'd

left. 'He's glad to have some peace and quiet. Now, tell me about school.'

Polly filled her in on the details and answered her queries while Pat devoured the bun with a look of pleasure on her face.

Polly was impressed that she knew most of the families whose children were at school.

'Oh, and I met Walter and . . .'

'Nancy? Delightful woman. They used to work at the Hall, you know.'

Pat licked icing off her fingers and Polly saw the swollen joints. They looked painful.

'Yes, they told me. I was out for a walk at the weekend and stopped to chat with them. They said how much they appreciated being allowed to stay in the lodge.'

'We couldn't bear to move them on. In any case, we don't need as much accommodation for the workers now.'

They continued to chat. Pat moved the conversation on to when she and her husband both worked and how much they'd loved it.

Polly seized her chance.

'I know Richard was very hands-on with outdoor work. In fact, I was looking at the photos hanging up in the potting shed.

'Someone mentioned he helped clean out the pond at the end of each season but I'm not sure if he was in any of them.'

'I think he would be. Much younger, of course. That's maybe why you didn't recognise him.'

She hollered to the closed door.

'Richard!'

A few seconds later the door opened.

'Did you call me?'

'Yes, love. Could you bring me a couple of the photo albums from the bookcase in your study. I want to show Polly what you looked like as a young man.'

'I haven't changed a bit!'

He swept his hand over his receding hairline, making them all laugh, and returned a minute later with several albums.

At the Beach

Everything was ready for Steve's arrival on Wednesday. The food was in the oven, plates were warming and the table was set.

She loved that he was always punctual so she was confident the food wouldn't spoil.

'Something smells good!' His nostrils twitched as he wiped his feet on the mat.

'Salmon en croûte with roasted vegetables.' She had discovered Steve would eat anything and that he had a healthy appetite.

'My tummy's rumbling just thinking about it.' He patted his flat stomach.

'First things first; there's something I want to show you.' She took his hand and led him through the house, throwing open the back door.

Steve's eyebrows shot up and a smile spread across his face. He stepped outside, stood in the middle of the decking and made a 360-degree turn.

'I like it!'

'Really?' Was he just being polite?

'Honest. I couldn't have planned it better myself.'

'I did all the things you said so it was you who planned it, actually.'

'Well, I didn't suggest the bird-bath, nor the sun-catchers. What a difference! Well done.' He gave her a big hug.

A warm glow of satisfaction washed over her at such praise. She gave him a final squeeze then stepped back.

'Come on, let's eat. We can have coffee outside afterwards, if it's not too cold, and gaze at my wonderful creation.'

'That's a sound plan.'

During the meal Polly gave a blow-by-blow account of her transformation of the garden, including the trip to the reclamation yard. She didn't mention seeing Dennis.

'That was delicious, as always.' Steve dabbed the corners of his mouth with his serviette. 'I'll clear up if you'd like to make coffee and we can catch the last of the sun.

'I want to inspect — I mean admire — what you've done in the garden.'

Polly gave him a playful slap before gathering together the coffee things. She adored these evenings, with the two of them completely at ease with other.

She even dared to think that they were like an old married couple.

'I have a bit of a dilemma,' Steve confessed when Polly placed the tray on the table.

The sun was sinking, casting a kaleidoscope of colours on the fence and decking from the twirling sun-catchers.

'What's that?' Polly kept her voice light but a jumble of thoughts raced through her mind, none of them positive.

'It seems my work at Izzy's has not gone unnoticed. Her neighbour two doors along would like my services, too.'

'So what's the dilemma?'

'If I take it on it means I would have to forgo Wednesday evenings. That's our evening.'

Polly considered.

'I could always come along to Izzy's,

or Mum and Dad's, when you're there.'

It wouldn't be quite the same but she understood the extra money came in handy. It would mean she would get to see him, at least.

'Would you mind very much? We'd still have every other weekend for just the two of us.'

'Of course I don't mind.'

It was good to see Steve's confidence returning even if it was at the cost of their time together.

Come the shorter days of winter they would have the evenings together because he wouldn't then be able to work in the dark.

'Talking of weekends, how would you like to spend the afternoon with me and Freya on Saturday?'

'I'd like that very much.'

He squeezed her hand.

'Good, that's settled. I'll think of where we could go. The beach or the park if it's dry, somewhere indoors if it's raining.'

* * *

On Friday Polly consulted the weather app on her phone and discovered it was due to be sunny next day. She offered to make a picnic.

Steve's reply included a list of Freya's food likes and dislikes which were typical of a six-year-old.

Polly went into the hardware store next morning and bought a bucket and spade, just in case.

When they arrived to pick her up Polly invited them indoors. Freya bounded in and went from room to room.

'Sorry about this,' Steve said. 'She's very nosy.'

Polly smiled.

'I don't mind.'

'Your house is really small,' Freya announced when she'd finished exploring.

'Freya, don't be rude,' Steve admonished.

'But it is!' She looked unabashed.

'You're quite right, Freya. It is small,

but I quite like it this way,' Polly told her. 'Now, would you like to carry the picnic blanket? Daddy can carry the basket.'

Freya skipped out to the car and soon they were on their way.

The afternoon was filled with fun and there were no awkward moments. Not only had Steve packed some sand toys, he'd also brought a soft-ball tennis set, football and kite, all of which were put to good use.

In fact, the only time they sat down was to eat. Freya was an easy-going child and a pleasure to be around. It was testament to her upbringing.

At one point Polly caught Steve watching her as she interacted with Freya, a smile on his face. She wondered what was going through his mind and if she'd passed the test, if there was one.

When he dropped her off and Freya gave her a big hug, saying it had been the best day ever, Polly knew it was a big change in their relationship.

She hoped she could now broach the subject of dodgy Dennis with him.

Unwelcome News

Over the next few weeks Polly's life, apart from school and the café, slipped into a pattern. When Steve was working at Izzy's Polly walked the short distance so that she could, at least, be in the same place as him.

It gave her a chance to have some time with Izzy, too. She was fairly sure her aunt could manage the garden on her own again but she seemed to enjoy Steve's professional touch.

Polly also went with Steve to her parents' house when he was due there.

The nights were drawing in. In another month or so he'd have to finish up earlier which would give them back some time in the evenings together.

It meant he would have to sacrifice part of his weekend but, knowing Steve, he wouldn't allow it to impact on his time with Freya.

The October school holidays were looming and Polly still hadn't booked anything. It wasn't like her to procrastinate but something was holding her back.

Perhaps it was the fear that another letter would arrive at the school to hurry up the closure process.

'You'll see me at the Hall tomorrow afternoon.' Izzy elbowed Polly as she passed her an empty mug to take indoors. 'I love this time of year with the leaves changing colour. I want to see the big splash of amber and russet in the woodland near the walled garden.'

'I'll be sure to keep a scone for you, in that case. The trees do look lovely, don't they, Steve?'

Polly had noticed that he was quieter than usual. Sometimes it was difficult to get a word in edgeways when Izzy was around but now and again she had caught him staring into space.

Something was wrong.

Steve looked from one to the other. '

'Oh, sorry, I hadn't realised you were speaking to me.' His face broke into a smile. 'Yes, the trees really are beautiful.

You must come and see them, Izzy.'

Later, when Steve dropped her off at her house, she undid her seatbelt and swung round to face him.

'Something's up, Steve, I can tell. If I've done . . . ?'

He pulled her into his embrace and kissed the top of her head.

'It isn't you. It could never be you.'

Polly felt his warm breath as he let out a big sigh.

She pulled back and looked him in the eye.

'What is it, then? I can tell you're troubled.'

Steve bowed his head and gripped her hands.

'This afternoon Dennis came to tell me I have to move out.'

'What? He can't do that, can he?'

What a cruel, nasty trick! Was this an act of revenge for Polly befriending Pat? Turning her boyfriend out into the street.

No, that was too far-fetched.

'He says he's going to advertise the cottages as Airbnbs. Apparently it's part of his strategy to make more money for the Hall.'

Polly could feel her jaw tighten.

'That man is not going to get away with this!'

Steve squeezed her hands.

'Please, Polly, don't make waves. It'll only make things worse for me. I need that job.

'I'll just find somewhere else to live.'

Yes, somewhere unaffordable, and that only if he could find somewhere. There was nothing available in Heatherton as far as Polly knew.

She wasn't sure if there were any suitable properties in Dalcleish, either. If not, what would happen?

Would it mean he'd have to move away? She couldn't bear the thought.

From what she knew about his former in-laws they were decent folk and would, no doubt, offer him a place to stay. The trouble was they lived a long way away.

She felt a crushing feeling across her chest. There was only one thing for it. She took a deep breath and closed her eyes.

'Steve, remember once before I tried to tell you I had my suspicions about Dennis?'

'Look, Polly,' Steve began.

'No, Steve, this time you have to listen.'

Polly told him about having seen Dennis at the reclamation yard on two occasions. He raised his eyebrows as she related that the first time had been when they were there together buying Izzy's chimney-pot.

She told Steve about having witnessed Dennis selling a piece that she was certain belonged to the hall.

She described the time she had discovered the items hidden under the tarpaulin and how they'd disappeared the day after Dennis had caught her.

Finally she told him about befriending Pat Aitken and how, in an old photograph, she had seen the item he'd been selling.

'I'm not sure I should get involved.' This sounded more like the old Steve, the one whom Polly had met at first.

Who wouldn't say boo to a goose.

'You are involved — your home is about to be taken from you. I can't stand back and watch it happen, nor can I let Dennis ruin things for that lovely couple.

'I've got to know them quite well and I have a feeling they'd love to get their teeth into the Hall's activities but are afraid to overstep the mark.

'It's ridiculous — they own the place!'

She looked at him.

'Are you with me on this?'

Steve thought for a moment.

'I suppose I've nothing more to lose but my job and, if it came to it, I'm sure I'd get something else. Yes, I'm in.'

Polly nodded.

'Thank goodness. When did Dennis say you've to quit the cottage?'

'I have to be out by Christmas.'

'Oh, Steve, talk about heartless! Have you spoken to any of your neighbours to find out how they feel about it?'

'Not had a chance yet. None of them work at the Hall so they don't have the same vested interest that I do.'

Polly's first thought had been whether the Aitkens knew about this. She was sure it would be unwelcome news.

Pat cared about the tenants but would she challenge Dennis about it?

Then would Dennis ask where she got her information from?

Polly and Steve would have to be careful. One false move and Dennis could see them both out on their ear.

'It might be best not to say anything for the moment. You and I are going to uncover Dennis's misdeeds before he does any further damage.'

'Do you have a plan?'

'To be honest, no, I'm just making it up as I go along. One thing that would be helpful is to find out where he moved the stuff to after the outbuilding. Any ideas?'

'Afraid not. We gardeners don't have access to all the buildings, some of which are locked. It could be anywhere.

'Were there a lot of things? I mean could he have moved it far all by himself?'

'Good point.'

It hadn't crossed Polly's mind until now that maybe Dennis had had help to move the stuff. He was notoriously lazy. If he did have help, who was it?

Three Little Words

The next time they were at her parents' house Polly let slip the news of Steve's imminent eviction. The talk was of where to plant spring bulbs and Polly muttered he might not be there to see them.

'What? That's terrible, Steve! You can stay with us, no question.'

Polly's mum came outdoors.

'Is something wrong, dear?'

'Steve's going to be homeless. I said he can stay with us as long as he likes. That's all right, isn't it?'

'Of course, we have plenty of room.'

She put her hand on Steve's arm.

'Assuming you're not inviting him to stay with you, that is.' Jim looked at Polly whose face turned red.

She and Steve hadn't had that conversation.

He saved her from further embarrassment. 'It's so kind of you but I hope to find somewhere soon for Freya to come.

'I really do appreciate it though.'

'You can tell my dad is no diplomat, can't you?' Polly remarked to Steve later, glad of the descending dusk to hide her blushes.

They were in his car outside her house.

'I'm sorry he put us on the spot like that.'

'It was a fair assumption, don't you think? We've been seeing each other for months.'

'Yes, but he shouldn't have come out with it like that.'

She'd day-dreamed about sharing her life with him one day, when he was ready. She knew that she was but the suggestion had to come from him.

Polly didn't want to push him into anything especially since any decisions he made would affect Freya. Nor did she want to knock his confidence.

'I care very much about you, Polly.'

He looked straight ahead into the back of the car parked in front, picking at his fingernails. Was he about to tell her that it had been a blast but . . . ?

She mustn't cry. She must hold it together till he'd said his piece. Then she'd run inside and allow herself to bubble like a baby.

Suddenly he swung round, took her face in his hands and looked into her eyes.

'I love you, Polly.'

She closed her eyes, accepted his tender kiss and tried to ignore the two fat tears that rolled down her cheeks.

'I love you, too,' she replied shakily.

'I've wanted to tell you that for some time.' He was back to staring ahead. 'The thing is, I have nothing to offer you.

'As you know I lost everything. I'm nowhere near back on my feet and don't know when I will be.'

He smiled.

'I've been lucky thanks to you arranging for me to do work for your parents and Izzy. The extra money has been brilliant.'

He turned away again.

'But now I'm having to find somewhere

else to live.' He shook his head.

She took his hand.

'You know my mum and blabber-mouth dad are serious. Don't discount their offer to stay with them until you can find somewhere.'

Steve chuckled.

'I know. I'm very touched.'

'It might be your safest bet,' Polly warned. 'Once Izzy knows she's liable to lasso you next time you're there and demand you stay with her!'

It was good to end the conversation on a light note.

Steve had his pride and Polly respected that, but it made her even more determined that Dennis should get his comeuppance.

Artist Daughter

Polly would often pop upstairs after the café closed. She and Pat would chat whilst indulging in Mrs McTavish's daily treat.

'You must tell me where you're going in the holidays,' Pat enthused. 'I'll miss your company but I look forward to hearing all about it.

'I think you were going to book a cycling or walking holiday which sounds like fun.'

'Yes. I'm torn between the Lake District and the Yorkshire Dales.'

Pat's gaze was dreamy.

'Both are beautiful. You could always do one this year and the other next year. Actually, our Hazel spent a summer in the Dales. As an au pair, would you believe, for a farming family.

'There were lots of children and it was a bit chaotic but she loved it. She did several paintings of the surrounding moorland, and one or two of little villages she visited.

'There's one in the hallway. If you're swaying between them both it might help you decide.'

She followed her intrigued visitor into the hall. Pat was a bit quicker on her feet these days, Polly noticed, and seemed less stiff when she moved.

'That's it.'

Pat pointed to a pleasing landscape with subtle shades of lilac and green under a moody sky. A white farmhouse and tall barns nestled in the crease of two hills.

'Is that where she worked?'

'Yes,' Pat replied. 'She loves the country. That's why I was surprised when she settled in London.'

'She obviously made a success of it otherwise she wouldn't have stayed there.'

'Yes. When she first went there she immersed herself in the art scene. It was more alluring than anything up here.'

'Does she have a studio?'

'She can't afford to maintain a

permanent studio so she does a pop-up one now and again to exhibit ,and sell her work.

'She paints at her home. It wouldn't suit me at all but it works for her.'

Polly gazed at the painting, deep in thought.

'I suppose I should show you a painting of the Lake District so you can make an informed decision.'

'No need, I've made up my mind.'

'That's just as well — Hazel never visited the Lake District.'

Secret Plan

'Did you say you're going to London?' Polly and Steve were walking the 'loop' path, as they now called it, from the Hall to Heatherton village and back, so there was no chance of anyone overhearing them.

'Yes, I did, and that's strictly between you and me. Please don't go telling anyone.

'As far as my parents, work colleagues and everyone else know I'm travelling to the Yorkshire Dales for a cycling holiday.'

'Why London?' he pressed.

'That's where Pat and Richard's daughter lives. I'm hoping to see her.'

It sounded simple when Polly said it but she was terrified at the thought it could all go horribly wrong.

Steve shook his head, clearly trying to make sense of this.

'Exactly why are you going there to see her?'

'I think Hazel might be the key to

sorting out the mess at the Hall. I've kind of built up a profile of her through conversations with Pat and I believe she'll listen to me.

'I'm hoping to get the opportunity to tell her about what Dennis is up to and how I fear for what he might do next.

'The best outcome would be that she felt strongly enough about it to come home and speak with her mum and dad and then help them find someone more suitable to run things.'

Steve took a sharp intake of breath.

'London's a big place. Do you even know where she lives? You're not intending to turn up on her doorstep, are you?'

'Not exactly. I did a Google search and found her online so I know which area she lives in.

'There was an enquiry form on her website which I completed to say I'd be interested in seeing some of her work. Apparently appointments can be made by arrangement.'

'Get you, Miss Marple! Have you rehearsed what you're going to say to her? Your opening line had better be good or she might call the cops immediately.'

'More or less, plus I've got a six-hour train journey to learn my spiel off by heart!'

'You've bought tickets already?'

Polly nodded.

'I've also booked a cheap — and hopefully cheerful — hotel for three nights. The expense is eating into my savings, unfortunately, and they're my emergency fund for if the school closes.

'Mind you, Marjory's convinced a fairy is going to wave her magic wand. Anyway, if this helps to topple Dennis it'll be money well spent.'

'You've got a big heart, Polly.'

Steve climbed over a stile and offered his hand to help her over.

'It's one of the reasons I love you.'

She stepped down on to the path and straight into Steve's open arms. He hadn't stopped uttering the 'L' word ever since he'd first used it and she never tired of hearing it.

★ ★ ★

The children were very excited on the last day of term so little work was done. It suited Polly who couldn't concentrate either. Her nerves were at fever pitch.

At lunchtime Marjory and Clare wished her a good holiday.

'Send us some pics,' Clare urged.

'I'm not sure I'll have time,' Polly replied. 'It's going to be pretty full on. Besides the paperwork said we'd often be in areas with poor reception.'

'Well, we can see them when you get back.'

Polly would worry about that when the time came. She could always pretend she accidentally deleted the images.

She was due holidays from the café so she booked time off there. Fortunately, Dennis wasn't interested in what she would be doing with her time off.

He was probably glad to have her out of the way. Her presence seemed to put him on edge, as if he knew she was on to him.

She visited Pat the day before her departure.

'I almost feel like I'm going with you. I've got some things for you.'

Pat pointed to some leaflets on the table between them. The pictures on them looked straight out of 'All Creatures Great And Small'.

'We never throw anything away. Everywhere we used to go we collected leaflets and brochures and filed them away when we came home. These are from a holiday years ago.

'Many of them will be outdated but the places are still the same. If you've room for them they might come in handy.'

Polly leafed through them, pausing to read certain sections.

'These are super, Pat, thanks for looking them out. I'll put these in my backpack and I'll look out for some of the sights if they're close to the cycling track.'

She realised she was going to have to fabricate an awful lot of stories!

'It's a big area and you may be miles

away, of course. Where does the route take you?'

Polly thought quickly.

'I did look at the map but I've already forgotten the names of the villages and towns we go through. All I know is I get off the train at Harrogate and a mini-bus picks me up and takes me to the starting point.'

'You're so brave, going on your own.' Pat looked envious.

'I won't be on my own really. There will be other people doing the same thing.'

'Well, I still think it's very exciting. Oh, to be young and adventurous!'

Polly stood up and put the leaflets in her bag.

'I'll tell you all about it when I get back.'

She was beginning to believe the story herself.

When she got home she slipped the leaflets into a drawer, on top of the new cycling gloves and vest her mum had given her especially for this trip.

'Stop feeling guilty about it,' she lectured herself as she crammed her backpack with clothes for three days. 'This is for the greater good.'

Down in the Smoke

The train pulled out of the station and picked up speed. Polly stared out of the window, baffled at what she was doing.

People came and went and she ate her packed lunch, going over in her mind all the things she would say to Hazel.

Eventually they trundled through the London suburbs and she began to pick out iconic landmarks. She disembarked at King's Cross and travelled west by Tube, the butterflies in her tummy multiplying.

When she reached her stop she climbed up to street level, unprepared for the noise, and after consulting her A-Z walked the couple of blocks to her hotel where she was greeted by a pleasant young man on reception who directed her to her room.

It was tiny but a welcome sight. She slung her backpack on to the chair and collapsed on the bed which creaked beneath her. Hopefully she'd be so tired she'd sleep through the unfamiliar sounds of the night.

She reached into her pocket for her phone and dialled. It rang twice.

'Polly! How was the journey?'

'Uneventful. Amazing how tired you can feel after doing nothing all day!' She paced the room. 'How are you?'

'Missing you and worried about you there on your own. You don't have to do this.'

'We both know I do. I'll stay in touch.'

'Have you arranged a place to meet her?'

'Yes, a church hall a couple of Tube stops from here. Some of her work is on display there. I've to be there at two tomorrow.'

'Make sure it's in a well-lit area.'

'It'll be broad daylight!' She stifled a giggle.

'Then make sure it's not up a dark alleyway. Phone me if you feel . . .'

'Steve, you've been reading too many crime novels.'

'I don't want anything to happen to

194

you, that's all.'

'Tell you what, when I reach the building I'll take a photo and send it to you. I assure you if I'm in any doubt I won't go in.'

She could sense his relief.

'Good. I have to go, I'm due at Izzy's.'

'And I need something to eat. The room service menu is very uninspiring but I can't face going out again.

'By the way, Izzy will probe you about my holiday. Don't be caught off guard.'

'You've no fear on that score. I've also rehearsed what I've to say if asked.'

Finding Hazel

The church wasn't at all what Polly had expected. Of modern design, it was built in light-coloured stone with sleek lines and lots of glass, including a stunning stained-glass window overlooking the street.

She took a photograph and sent it to Steve with the message. *I'm going in.*

Then she switched off her phone and put it in her pocket.

The church hall was an annexe at the rear of the building with the same contemporary feel. Taking a deep breath Polly pushed the door open and stepped inside to the warmth and smell of home baking.

Through the glass partition she could see people milling around the open space. At one end was a coffee bar with chairs and tables set out, many of them occupied.

A mini library stood against the far wall with shelves of books and soft seating.

As she strolled around the hall nearly all those Polly passed smiled at her, putting her at ease. It was clear the hall was well used.

A notice board held drawings by Sunday school children. Another had notices of all manner of groups: mother and toddlers; seniors; Brownies and walking group.

The far wall was devoted entirely to framed paintings and Polly found Hazel wasn't the only one displaying work judging by the variety of styles.

One of the walled garden at Heatherton Hall caught her eye. Captured in summer it was a riot of colourful borders.

In the foreground was an apple tree laden with fruit. Hazel had even captured the bench upon which Polly often sat to have lunch.

'Excuse me, are you Polly?' The smooth tones came from the right.

Polly turn around and looked directly into the smiling face of a younger version of Pat. She had the same shape of face, eye colour and warm smile.

'Yes, I am. You must be Hazel.'

Hazel looked surprised and bemused at the sound of her voice.

'You're Scottish! So am I.'

'I know.'

Polly could have slapped herself. She'd had along train journey and a whole night to practise this moment and yet the first thing she had done was put her foot in it.

Hazel's puzzled face cleared.

'Oh, the website? I give far too much away. Anyway, it's nice to meet you, Polly, and thanks for your interest in my work.'

'I really like your paintings. I feel like I can step right into them.'

That much was not made up.

'That's exactly what an artist likes to hear. Let me show you the others, then I'll leave you to browse in your own time.'

Polly listened as Hazel explained each picture, telling her what the scene was. She kept quiet even though she recognised another two settings from the Hall.

Hazel turned to Polly.

'Look, I don't want to do the hard sell so I'll step away and leave you. If you fancy a cuppa I won't be far away.

'It would be nice to have a chat with a fellow Scot.'

There was something about Hazel's easy manner that emboldened Polly. She decided to spit it out before she bottled it.

Her heart pounding, she swallowed hard.

'Do you know something? I'd really like to have that cuppa now — if that's OK.'

'Sure. I can't wait to hear some tales of home.'

Some of them you won't believe.

Hazel insisted on buying, making Polly feel even more guilty.

'Spoiler alert,' Hazel said as she deposited the paper cups on the table. 'The coffee isn't great but that's not the point of this place.'

She handed Polly a paper plate containing a generous slice of chocolate cake.

'I can recommend the baking, though.'

'Told you,' she remarked when Polly grimaced at the first sip of coffee. 'So tell me, Polly, where do you live? Your accent is familiar but I'm pretty hopeless at placing people.'

Polly watched Hazel take a big mouthful of cake. It would, hopefully, give her just enough time to get over the gist of why she was here today.

'I live in Dalcleish and I'm a Support for Learning Assistant at Heatherton school. I work part-time in the café at the Hall to supplement my income.'

Hazel froze, a lump of cake making her cheek bulge. Out of her peripheral vision Polly could see the door. It looked very inviting.

Hazel set her plate down on the table and began to chew slowly, her smile gone and replaced by a furrowed brow.

This wasn't going according to plan. In fact, it was a disaster. She should never have come.

Hazel wiped her mouth on her serviette and gave Polly a curious look.

'Why are you here, Polly?'

'I'm concerned for your mum and dad.'

Hazel sat up sharply.

'Why, what's wrong with them?'

'There's nothing wrong with them,' Polly assured her. 'I saw your mum the other day and she is looking and keeping very well.

'My reason for coming here is that I want to tell you about Dennis.'

'Dennis?'

'The manager at the Hall.'

Polly was surprised she didn't seem to recognise the name.

'What about him?' Hazel sat back and folded her arms.

Polly recounted all she had planned to say, leaving out nothing. She tried to ignore the different expressions on Hazel's face which ranged from scepticism to surprise and possibly anger.

When she'd finished Hazel picked up her coffee cup, looked at the contents, then put it down again.

'Do Mum and Dad know you're here?'

'Absolutely not!'

Polly's raised voice caused others to turn around and she lowered it.

'The only person who knows I'm here is my boyfriend. He's a gardener at the Hall and is one of the people who are going to be made homeless come Christmas.

'That's not the reason I came. In fact he didn't want me to come. Thing is, I've seen so much while working in the café.

'It's clear to me that Dennis is helping himself to things that belong at the Hall. The working atmosphere is strained and Mrs McTavish tells me it's nothing like it was in the old days.'

A smile lit up Hazel's face.

'Dear Mrs McTavish. Is she still working all hours?'

Polly nodded and smiled, too.

'She is and she's certainly wise to Dennis. Since your mum started to invite me upstairs for chats with her Mrs McTavish has hinted to me that it would be a good thing if she got to hear about Dennis's misdeeds.'

'But you haven't told Mum?'

'No. Through our conversations I've learned that your parents were grateful to him for taking on the job when your mum's health wasn't good.

'I know they don't want to interfere — they've said as much — but I get the impression they'd love to get involved in running the Hall again.'

'That's why you've come to see me?'

'I couldn't think what else to do.'

For the first time since she'd left home Polly felt as though a big weight had been lifted from her.

'Are you telling me you came all the way to London just to tell me all this?'

'Yes! I was hoping you might be able to intervene — see Dennis on his way and help your parents get someone more suitable. Someone who won't steal things.

'Who would nurture the business and the workers. Who could help your parents get involved in running things again. I know how much they miss it.'

Hazel looked pensive.

'How long are you here for, Polly?'

'Two more nights, then I get the train back the following morning.'

'Would you like to have dinner with me and my family tomorrow at my house?'

She hadn't blown it, after all!

'That would be lovely, thank you.'

'Good. It will give me time to explain things to my daughter and son-in-law.

'Meet me back here at four o'clock and we'll get the Tube together. I live not far from here.'

'I'll see you then. Can I ask just one thing? Please don't mention this to your parents yet.

'Your mum thinks I'm on a cycling holiday in the Yorkshire Dales!'

Busy Household

Early next morning Polly took the Tube, crammed with commuters, into the centre of London. She wanted to see as much as she could before meeting Hazel.

Yesterday had gone well and her heart felt so much lighter having unburdened herself.

She walked for miles, taking in the tourist sights like Big Ben and the Houses of Parliament. When she'd been in London as a schoolgirl she'd been more interested in the clothes shops and fast-food outlets.

She ate a sandwich sitting on a bench in Hyde Park, glad to have some distance between her and the constant sound of traffic, then strolled along myriad paths until it was time to join Hazel.

'Everyone's looking forward to meeting you,' Hazel said, pulling on her coat.

'Do you exhibit in other places?' Polly asked as they travelled the short journey.

'I've a few pieces in different outlets;

hotels, restaurants, a couple of art shops. They don't lead to huge sales but I also do commissions and give art classes.'

'You obviously love it here.'

Hazel frowned.

'I did at first; it was worlds away from my childhood home. I met an artist, fell in love, married, had my daughter then divorced.'

'I'm sorry.'

'We were arguing all the time. It wasn't good for any of us.'

'Did you consider going home?'

'That would have been the easy option but I wanted to prove to my parents I could stand on my own two feet. Besides, I didn't want to stop my daughter seeing her dad.

'Years passed and Rose, that's my daughter, grew up and got married. She moved her husband in with us and soon there were three children filling the house with laughter and chaos!'

She turned to Polly and smiled.

'Don't say you haven't been warned. Right, this is our stop.'

Polly fell in step with Hazel as they chatted and weaved their way through residential streets until Hazel steered her up a short path and unlocked the door.

'Granny!' A little girl dressed in school uniform raced towards her and threw her arms around Hazel's legs.

She was followed by another girl who could have been her twin. Taking up the rear was a tousle-haired boy. The three jumped up and down as Granny hugged each one.

It was a heart-warming scene.

'This is Granny's friend, Polly,' Hazel told them. 'Say hello.'

'Hello, Polly!' they chorused then raced down the narrow hallway.

'What a lovely way to be greeted every day!' Polly remarked.

'It is,' Hazel agreed. 'Come through.'

They hung their coats on the hallstand and followed the sound of voices to the kitchen. The youngsters were seated at the table, tucking into fish fingers, chips and beans.

A woman around Polly's age was filling

the dishwasher whilst encouraging the children to eat.

'Hi, Mum. You must be Polly? I'm Rose.'

'Nice to meet you, Rose.'

'Take a seat and I'll make some coffee. We'll eat later once this lot are in bed.'

'I can make the coffee.' Hazel filled the kettle and gathered the things together.

Polly sat on the sofa at the far end of the kitchen with a view through to the back garden. It was the width of the ter-raced house, separated from the gardens on either side by a big hedge.

The garden was all grass, bald in places with a climbing frame, a swing and a goal post. Polly couldn't help but think of the contrast to the rambling gardens at the Hall.

While she drank her coffee Hazel and Rose busied themselves with chores. Despite noise and squabbles it was good natured.

Rose disappeared with the girls to do homework and Hazel bathed her grandson.

In between all the activity she met Rose's husband, Mike, who made fresh coffee for them both and slumped in a nearby seat.

He looked weary. Polly learned he worked in sales for a phone company and he made it clear he and Rose couldn't manage without Hazel.

When the others returned Hazel magically produced a dish she had prepared the night before and which she had heated in the oven earlier.

They all sat down to eat and enjoy the bottle of wine that Polly had brought.

Hazel let out along sigh.

'At last we've got some peace to talk. Polly, I have explained everything to Mike and Rose. We're all concerned naturally about what's going on up there.

'Mum and Dad have never let on that they were worried about things. We just assumed everything was fine, though I haven't been home since Mum's condition worsened.

'The three of us think it best I pay a visit as soon as possible and try to get to the bottom of things.'

Rose and Mike nodded in agreement but left all the talking to Hazel.

Polly couldn't have asked for more. Despite her soft exterior there was an inner strength to Pat's daughter and Polly was confident she'd be able to put things right.

'Your parents will be so pleased to see you, your mum especially. She talks so often about you and is very proud when she shows off your work.'

Hazel waved away the compliment.

'Mum and Dad are so independent that it wouldn't cross their minds to ask me or my sister for help. Polly, I'm really grateful to you for coming all this way to tell me.

'I won't, of course, let on that you said anything to me.'

Polly was less worried about that now. Hazel had believed her and she, in turn, now believed Dennis's days at the Hall were numbered.

'Thank you. I'll have to concoct a good story about my cycling adventures in Yorkshire, mind!

'I might need to acquire a few scratches and bruises for good effect.'

All four of them burst out laughing.

Hopeful

After her return to Dalcleish Polly kept a low profile for the first few days.

As far as her parents and Izzy were concerned she was wanting to recharge her batteries after a gruelling few days of cycling.

She laid it on very thick, saying the route had been very hilly and that her few miles of flat cycling every day hadn't quite cut it as adequate training.

Fortunately Polly's mum and dad were busy preparing for their next trip. Otherwise they would have been round to check she was all right.

Steve dropped in to see her on his way home from Izzy's neighbour. This was on the same day she got back.

She hadn't realised how much she'd missed him until their eyes locked and she was in his arms.

'So, when's Hazel coming here?'

Steve sat down on the sofa beside her. He looked tired. She guessed the threat of being made homeless was causing him anguish.

'Early next week, she said. She has a few things to organise before she leaves.

'She also wanted to give her mum and dad a bit of warning rather than just turn up on their doorstep.'

'Do you really believe she can sort things out?' he asked.

Polly took his hands and faced him directly.

'Oh, Steve, I really do believe that. What hadn't dawned on me until I was there was that Hazel is the heir to the Hall!

'It was the little comments she dropped into conversation when I had dinner with them that made me realise that one day she was always going to return.

'She spoke about going home sooner than she'd anticipated. I know she wasn't talking about just a weekend break.'

He squeezed her hands.

'I hope you're right.'

'I do, too.'

* * *

Marjory's brow furrowed as Polly told her and Clare on Monday morning that she hadn't any photos of the holiday to show them.

She explained that they were all cycling individually and there had never been an opportunity.

'What? Not even for a selfie?'

Marjory and Clare looked at each other and then at her in disbelief.

Polly put up a convincing counter argument, she hoped.

'Every time I stopped it was either to eat, go to the loo or catch my breath. I'm afraid it never crossed my mind to get my phone out and capture the moment!'

Clare shrugged.

'Ah, well. Did you have a nice break anyway?'

'Yes, I did. It made up for not getting away in the summer.'

'Summer! Next thing we know we'll be rehearing for the Christmas show.'

Marjorie gave a sigh and Polly guessed

she was probably thinking that it might well be the last one for the school. The three of them would be out of a job.

That was the least of Polly's worries just now.

She found it ironic that she'd taken the job at the Hall to bank some money should that happen yet now her biggest headache was to help sort out the shenanigans at the Hall.

However, with Hazel in the frame, she felt the stirrings of hope.

Surprise Visitor

Polly had almost forgotten her so-called cycling holiday when, at lunchtime, she pedalled up the long drive to the café.

Her arrival clearly didn't go unnoticed by Pat who was waving cheerfully from the balcony.

'Hello, Polly! I hope you had a wonderful holiday.'

'It was great, thanks.' She got off the bike.

'I'm looking forward to hearing all about it. If you've got time after work do drop in.'

This was what Polly was afraid of.

'I'll do that. See you then.'

'Better you than me,' Mrs McTavish scoffed after asking and being told about the holiday. 'Can't remember the last time I was on a bike.'

'It's all right once you get used to it,' Polly assured her.

'I'd never get used to it! Oh, I must tell you — I'm so annoyed with myself.

Dennis caught me off guard last week and went off with half of a Victoria sandwich!'

He had gone off with a lot more than that, Polly thought.

'Never mind, I'm sure you'll make up for it this week,' she replied.

'Mark my words, I will.'

'By the way, Pat's invited me up after work today.'

The older woman whirled round as fast as her body would allow.

'Has she? That's good to hear. I'll make something nice for you to take and he . . .' she pointed to the office door ' . . .won't get so much as a sniff of it!'

Dennis slunk about all day as usual and looked crestfallen at the empty display cabinet when the café closed.

At five o'clock, with a bag of treats tucked under her arm, Polly climbed the stairs and was pleasantly surprised to see Pat waiting for her on the landing.

'You're looking well, Pat.'

Polly had never known the older woman to walk about on her own. She had a stick with her today but wasn't leaning on it as heavily as before.

Also, she seemed more upbeat than usual. Polly could guess why.

'I'm on different medication which is helping. Enough about me, though. It's good to see you, Polly. Come on in.

'Richard is making us a hot drink.'

'Well, Mrs McTavish has provided something to go with it.'

Polly was sure she heard the click of a door but when she looked back couldn't see anything. Naturally, she suspected that Dennis was eavesdropping.

After they'd eaten the iced currant buns and Polly had skimmed over the details of her 'holiday' Pat leaned in, a conspiratorial look on her face.

'I received some super news today.'

'Did you?'

'My daughter Hazel's coming up from London for a couple of weeks!'

'That's fantastic. She's the artist, isn't she? When's she coming?'

'She'll be here tomorrow, would you believe? The children are on school holidays and my granddaughter and her husband are taking them off somewhere so Hazel thought she'd spend some time up here.

'I'm looking forward so much to seeing her in the flesh. FaceTime isn't the same.'

Richard came in to collect the tray.

'Put the world to rights, have we?'

'I was telling Polly about Hazel coming to stay.'

'Isn't it wonderful? We'll have to think of some places to take her, I suppose.' He scratched his head.

'I rather think she's looking forward to some peace and quiet. She told me last night she was hoping to unwind and not to go organising things. She leads such a busy life down there.

'She wants to do some art while she's here. Oh, it'll be nice, just the two of us, sketching and painting together!'

Polly felt a pang of sadness at the thought of all the years Pat must have sorely missed her daughters.

'I'll make sure you meet her while

she's here, Polly,' Pat told her. 'I think you'll like her.'

'Thank you,' Polly said, knowing she would.

★ ★ ★

Hazel was the first person Polly saw when she went into the café next day. She had to remind herself they hadn't 'met'.

Hazel and Mrs McTavish were chatting away as she tried to slip past them to go behind the counter.

The older woman grabbed her arm.

'Polly, come and meet Pat and Richard's daughter, Hazel, here all the way from London.'

She turned and smiled.

'I can see the likeness. It's lovely to meet you, Hazel.'

'Lovely to meet you, too,' Hazel said.

'Polly works part-time here. She works at the school in the mornings.'

'How interesting.' Hazel smiled. 'That's my old school.'

'They're threatening to close it,'

Polly confided.

That subject hadn't come up when she was in London as it wasn't relevant to the whole Dennis situation.

'No! How dare they?'

Hazel looked indignant, then shook her head and laughed.

'Would you listen to me? I've been here five minutes at the start of what's supposed to be a relaxing holiday and I'm already stressed!

'It's great to see you again, Mrs McTavish. You'll see me often for some of your delicious home-baking. Polly, nice to meet you. Now I'm going for a walk around the garden and grounds.'

Mrs McTavish winked at Polly.

'Mark my words, she'll shake things up while she's here. It would be a very good thing if she got to hear about a certain someone and his antics.'

'Wouldn't it,' Polly said.

If only she knew.

A Cowardly Bully

By the time Hazel returned from her walk around the garden and grounds Polly was serving afternoon tea at an inside table.

Straight-faced, with determination in her step, Hazel rapped on Dennis's office door and went in without waiting for an answer.

There was a triumphant look on Mrs McTavish's face.

'Oh, to be a fly on that wall!'

Polly wished the same.

When Hazel emerged an hour later, a red-faced Dennis was at her heel and followed her outside like a puppy dog.

Next day, when Polly reached the café door at the start of her shift, Hazel and Dennis emerged from the outbuilding that was used as a store for café stock.

Dennis, brow beaded with perspiration, was jotting things down in a notebook.

Hazel looked like someone who was

on a mission and Polly longed to know what was going on.

Mrs McTavish gave her a naughty look.

'She's certainly keeping Dennis on his toes. He's running about like an errand boy!' She burst out laughing.

'That's what I like to hear, a happy workforce.' The voice was Hazel's as she descended the stairs.

'Enjoying your holiday, dear?' Mrs McTavish asked innocently.

Hazel leaned on the counter and sighed.

'I'm enjoying being back home, certainly, but I'm not sure about it being a holiday.'

She looked over her shoulder.

'You may have noticed I've been having short meetings with every employee here. May I steal Polly for a little while? We're not too busy today.'

'Of course, dear. Would you like a cup of coffee and a cake whilst you have your chat? I can get Amber to bring it to you.'

'Mrs McTavish, that would be

wonderful, thank you! It's been a long day.

'Polly, why don't you grab a table? I'll be right back. I just need to pick up my notes from upstairs.'

'Now, don't you hold back,' Mrs McTavish instructed when Hazel was out of earshot. 'I can't wait till she speaks to me!' She prodded her chest with her thumb.

Polly went outside and sat at the table furthest from the door, eagerly anticipating what she was going to be told.

'Haven't you got work to do?' Dennis barked as he approached from behind, making her jump to her feet and causing her heart to palpitate.

'I have a meeting.' Polly was annoyed with herself for sounding scared.

He looked at her with menace in his eyes. He was so close she could smell tobacco breath.

'Who would want to meet with an underling like you?'

'I would.' Hazel stood there.

He turned, red spots staining his

cheeks.

'I . . . I have to keep an eye on the workers. We have to keep up production.'

'Everyone is entitled to a break, Dennis. I would have thought that you'd know that since you're the manager.'

'Yes, yes, indeed. Well, I'll be off.' He backed away wearing a gormless grin.

'What a horrible man!' Hazel gave a little shiver. 'A bully and a coward.

'You were right, Polly. He is absolutely the wrong person for the Hall. It used to be such a happy place, too.

'There's no motivation now, no encouragement. If my parents knew . . .'

Her voice trailed off and she looked on the verge of tears.

'If there's anything I can do?' Polly begged.

'Thanks. You've done so much already. I'm kicking myself for believing all this time that Mum and Dad were making the best of retirement, thinking the business was in safe hands.'

'From what they've told me they were glad to have someone pick it up quickly so that your dad could concentrate on looking after your mum.

'They had no reason to doubt Dennis and they were distracted.'

'And there was me, so busy in London, working and helping to look after my grandchildren.' Hazel turned to Polly. 'I'm so glad you opened my eyes to this.

'It's up to me to put things right and I'm not leaving here until I've done that.'

★   ★   ★

'She said that?' Steve looked relieved as Polly relayed the news to him that evening. He had dropped in on his way home from yet another job further along Izzy's street.

Polly nodded.

'I'm not sure how quickly she can recruit another manager quickly, mind. After she sees Dennis off the premises, that is.'

'Did you ever find out what happened to the stuff under the tarpaulin?'

'Yes, I was about to tell you. Apparently the young apprentice gardener was asked by Dennis to move it into the old stables.

'Hazel found this out when she questioned him. The lad thought he was in trouble but she assured him otherwise.

'Hazel then got Dennis to show her inside all the other outbuildings, knowing they'd 'find' the stash. Dennis tried to tell her the items were surplus to requirements and were there for safe-keeping.'

'Did she ask him about the item you caught him selling?'

'Not yet. She wants to get as much information out of him as she can before she presents him with the photographic evidence I shared with her.'

'Was anything said about the use of the cottages?' Steve asked tentatively.

'I think the words she used were: 'Over my dead body will the current tenants be asked to leave. Airbnb indeed!''

Steve's shoulders visibly relaxed.

'Freya will be happy. She loves my cottage.'

'Hazel ordered Dennis to reverse that order immediately. Oh, and she was very annoyed that he'd neglected the hole in the outbuilding roof, saying it was now a much bigger and costlier job.

'I think you can say that Dennis's coat is on a shaky peg!'

Princess Freya

It was lovely to be spending Sunday with Steve and Freya. Polly's mind was consumed with thoughts of Dennis and of the monumental task Hazel faced, however.

She prayed there wouldn't be a loophole in Dennis's contract that meant they couldn't get rid of him.

'Can we go to soft play, Polly? Please?'

Freya took her hand and looked up at her. Polly had just arrived at the cottage.

'If Daddy says we can it's fine by me.'

'Polly says we can go!' Freya skipped through to the kitchen.

'Freya, what have I told you about playing us off against each other?' Steve remonstrated mildly as he kissed Polly. 'She does the same with me and her mum.'

'But I want to go to soft play!'

'We will but I told you maybe Polly might have suggestions, too.'

Polly pretended to think.

'Hmm. My suggestion is ... we do what Freya would like to do.'

'Hurray! I'll put my shoes on.'

Polly followed Steve into the kitchen. 'The soft play near here is better than where she lives, apparently. So, how are you today?' Steve scooped the remains of cereal into the food-waste bin.

'On tenterhooks. At least we know you're getting to stay here.'

'It's a weight off my shoulders, for sure.'

'Let's agree not to talk about the Hall today, for Freya's sake,' Polly suggested. 'She deserves your full attention.'

'I'm more than happy to do that. It's just nice to have a day off.' He gave a deep sigh.

'I feel partly responsible for that,' she apologised.

Arranging for him to help Izzy in her garden had spun out not only to her parents but also several of Izzy's neighbours. Somehow Steve was managing to accommodate them all.

'Don't get me wrong, I'm very grateful

for the extra cash. It's helped enormously towards getting me back on my feet.'

'I'm glad. Now, let's go off and enjoy the day.'

On cue Freya appeared in the doorway dressed in a pink, padded jacket with fur-lined hood. A glittery tiara was on her head.

'Princess Freya is ready and waiting so I think it's time to go.'

Taking Charge

Pat was looking jubilant while Richard's smile stretched from ear to ear. Polly had been invited to join them and Hazel, who would be returning to London the following day.

To Polly's dismay Dennis was still lurking in his office downstairs. She feared what action he might take after Hazel had disappeared.

Right now she put the bag of goodies from Mrs McTavish on the table. Pat rubbed her hands together in anticipation.

'Help yourself to milk,' Hazel offered, handing round mugs of coffee.

'I'm sorry I haven't invited you up here lately, Polly. It's just been so busy with Hazel here.

'We haven't done half as much painting as we had hoped but it has been for the very best of reasons.'

She looked conspiratorially across to Richard who took his wife's hand gently.

'That's right,' Richard continued. 'We had no idea that Hazel had come back to review the situation here, with the full intention of moving here and getting actively involved!'

Surprised, Polly looked at Hazel, whose face gave nothing away of what had gone between them.

'Permanently?'

Hazel nodded.

'I knew I would come back one day to take up the reins. Being here these past two weeks has made me realise how much I have missed it. I thought, why not do it now?'

'That's great! I'm sure your mum and dad are delighted.'

The news was just getting better and better, Polly reflected.

'We are,' Pat confirmed and Richard nodded firmly.

'Hazel, what about . . .' Polly almost blurted out the names of Rose, Mike and the children '. . . your job? That is, I assume you have a job in London.'

Gosh, she looked forward to the day

when she could stop telling lies!

'I'm self-employed so I just need to pick up my stock, which is on show in various places.

'My daughter and her family live in my house with me. All I'll I have to do is to arrange the transport of my personal things here.'

'Does this mean you will just start up your business again in this area?'

Polly was definitely in unfamiliar territory. Things had clearly moved on since they had last spoken.

'Yes, at least I will in time. Meanwhile I'm intending to take over the running of the Hall until we can employ another manager.'

Polly looked at the three of them and tried to form her next question. Her mouth had suddenly gone dry.

'Dear Dennis has decided to move on,' Pat said, rescuing her. 'The long commute has been getting to him, apparently, but he hadn't wanted to let us down.

'When he heard Hazel was returning he decided the time was right to move on to pastures new.'

'I see. That worked out well, then.'

Hurrah!

'I have to confess I'm looking forward to getting my hands dirty again,' Richard told her. 'I didn't like to tread on Dennis's toes.'

'And with my health so much improved you're going to be free to do that,' Pat reassured him.

'You can get your hands as dirty as you like, Dad,' Hazel promised. 'Some of the gardeners have been telling me how much they've missed you working alongside them.'

Polly listened to their excited chatter as if she was in a dream.

When the grandfather clock struck in the hall downstairs Hazel stood up and wiped the crumbs off her lap.

'Excuse me. I told Dennis I'd meet him now to collect his keys and to say goodbye to him.'

'I'd best be off, too.'

Polly rose, still desperate to know how Hazel had managed it.

On the landing Hazel leaned close and whispered.

'I'll ring you later and explain. You head off first.'

Polly was almost at the end of the drive when Dennis's car sped past, showering her with loose gravel. Her phone vibrated in her pocket so she stopped to take the call.

'Hi, Polly. That's him gone and good riddance!'

'If you don't mind me asking, how did you do it?'

'I kept my trump card — provided by you — until I made sure he'd provided me with all the digital files on his computer.

'When I was completely sure that he wouldn't be able to hold us to ransom I showed him the photograph.'

'Did he ask who had taken it?'

'Yes, but I didn't tell him. I asked what else he had sold off and he was surprisingly forthcoming. He told me he'd sold some stone plant tubs and a few statues.'

'Will you tell your parents?'

'No. I know those items have always belonged at the Hall but they don't care about things like that so I see no reason to say anything.

'As far as they're concerned Dennis has resigned and I'm taking over for the short term. They're overjoyed and I don't want to spoil that.'

'Again if you don't mind me asking, Hazel, at what point did you decide to move back here?'

Hazel shrugged.

'The magic of the Hall has lured me back as I knew, one day, it would. I'll miss seeing my grandchildren daily and it goes without saying that Rose will be cross, but I'll fight that battle tomorrow.'

Polly picked up her bike and rode home. She would share the news later with Steve when he dropped in on his way home from Izzy's house.

The thing she was most looking forward to was seeing Mrs McTavish's face tomorrow.

Uncertain Future

A couple of weeks passed with business at the Hall ticking away, organised from afar by Hazel. The atmosphere was much lighter and happier.

Richard, clad in old togs, was to be found here, there and everywhere, lending a hand where needed. The dirtier the job the better!

Polly assisted Pat in coming down in the lift one day for lunch at the café.

Mrs McTavish, who in Polly's eyes looked ten years younger these days, discarded her apron and sat down and joined her, leaving Polly and Amber in charge.

At school rehearsals began for the Christmas concert, reminding Polly that the year was ending and they were a step nearer possible closure.

She tried not to think about the children losing out on such a special primary experience and getting swallowed up by a much bigger school.

For herself, she was sure she could get full-time employment at the Hall. Hazel had hinted at bigger and better things but didn't say what they were.

But her heart lay in working with children.

One day a van reversed up to the front door and Hazel emerged. Polly rushed to the door just as Richard appeared from somewhere in the grounds.

'Welcome home, love.' He hugged her.

'Thanks, Dad.' Hazel opened the van's doors. 'All my worldly goods are here. I could do with a hand getting them inside.'

'I'll get a couple of the lads to help.'

Richard disappeared round the side of the building, leaving Polly and Hazel alone.

'What a difference it's been without Dennis, Hazel. You wouldn't believe it.'

'I'm sure I would. In the short time our paths crossed I saw him for what he was. He'll never be back, I can assure you.'

Hazel looked all around the large

hall with its high decorative ceiling and smiled.

'I can do so much more here than I ever could in London. I have plans for this place — but I won't be able to do them alone.'

Polly guessed that that was where a new manager would come in and she was confident Hazel would make very sure she appointed the right person.

A Life-Changing Decision

Next morning Polly was on playground duty when she spotted Hazel going into the lodge next to the school. She was greeted warmly by the old couple.

Over several days there was a flurry of activity as tradesmen turned up at the Hall.

'I expect she's going to get them to fix that roof,' Mrs McTavish said. 'She'll want to start up the art stuff again.'

'I think you're right,' Polly agreed.

'I haven't seen Pat and Richard look so happy in a long time.' The cook blinked rapidly. 'Makes me quite emotional just thinking about it.'

Hazel appeared with some empty cardboard boxes.

'That you finished unpacking, dear?'

Hazel dumped the boxes on the floor beside the gift-shop area.

'Yes, and I've found a good use for these.'

'What's that dear?'

241

'To put all this in!' Hazel indicated the stands and shelves stocked with mementoes. 'My vision for the future of the Hall does not include this rubbish!'

'Let me give you a hand,' Polly begged. 'If that's all right with you, Mrs McTavish.'

The older woman moved from behind the counter with astonishing swiftness.

'We're not busy just now. It would give me the greatest pleasure to help, too.'

When the full boxes had been loaded on to a trolley Polly and Hazel pulled it across the courtyard towards the old coach house.

'I've got something to tell you, Polly.'

'You're having the roof fixed?'

Hazel chuckled.

'Yes, but there's more news and I want you to hear it from me before it filters out. Especially since it's all down to you.'

Hazel sat down on top of a box and Polly sat opposite.

'Firstly, I was right. Rose was very angry with me and wouldn't speak to me for a whole day. She accused me of deserting them and said they couldn't possibly manage without me.

'Mike, the voice of reason, made her sit down that evening to talk it through. I'll cut to the chase. You won't believe this!'

'They're going to get a nanny?'

'Not even close. They're going to move up here, too!'

Polly's hand shot to her mouth.

'Gosh, that's a life-changer! It must have taken a lot of soul-searching.'

'Apparently, when Rose had calmed down it kind of all fell into place. In the end it was an easy decision for them to make.

'Mike is stressed out with his job and Rose spends half her working day travelling around London between venues, keeping her event-planning business afloat.

'I was the glue that was holding it all together. Collectively we were just existing.'

'What will they do up here for work?'

'I've asked Mike to be overall manager.

I know he'll be great at it and, let's face it, anything is an improvement on Dennis!

'Rose will start up her business and work from here. She's already buzzing with ideas for events at the Hall.'

A thought struck Polly.

'Is that why you were at the lodge the other day? To ask the occupants to leave so Rose and her family could move in?'

Hazel shook her head.

'No. I told them we would like to sell the lodge, to help finance some of the building work we're going to have to do to mend and refurbish some of the out-buildings.

'I gave them first refusal but they declined. They say they've wanted to move into sheltered accommodation for some time as the garden is far too big, but they didn't want to seem ungrateful to my mum and dad.

'The 'For Sale' sign is going up tomorrow.'

'Wow!' was all Polly could say.

'You haven't asked me about the most

important element in all this.'

Polly's brow furrowed.

'Maybe it's too much to take in in one go or I'm being dense.'

'The grandchildren,' Hazel hinted.

'What about them?'

Polly's eyes grew wider as the penny dropped.

'Two new school-age children in the village. You did say the school was at threat of closure because of declining pupil numbers, didn't you?'

'I did!' Polly was scarcely able to comprehend the news. 'This is incredible! Marjory, the head teacher, always believed that fate would intervene.'

'I couldn't agree more.'

'Gosh, I feel like crying.'

'Well, I feel like celebrating and once the family is all here we'll do just that.'

Polly groaned.

'It's bound to come out that I never went cycling, that I went to see you in London. What will your mum think?'

'She'll forgive you.'

'All's Well'

Steve hit the nail home and they stood back to admire the willow wreath on his door. A full moon cast a silvery blanket over everything. The trees twinkled with frost.

'Thanks for this, Polly. It was very generous of you.'

Polly had come directly from the Winter Extravaganza which had attracted hundreds of people, just as Hazel had predicted.

Her parents and Izzy had been there, too.

'Actually, I got it for nothing. Hazel insisted. They were selling like hot cakes — those and the handmade Christmas decorations.

'You should see the outbuilding. It's decked out with fake snow and Christmas trees all lit up. There are fun activities for the children.

'Rose was in charge of the whole thing. We must take Freya there at the weekend. She'll love it!'

'For sure.' He kissed Polly and she felt his cold nose against her cheek. 'Come on, let's get inside out of the cold.'

Mesmerised by the flickering flames they supped hot chocolate and wiggled their toes in front of the fire, each lost in their own thoughts.

'All's well that ends well,' Polly remarked with a contented sigh.

'What do you mean?' Steve studied her.

'Well, Dennis is history. Pat and Richard's house is bursting at the seams and Pat couldn't be happier. She and Hazel have advertised art classes for children as well as adults starting in the New Year. Rose has got all sorts of themed events planned throughout the year.

'Then there's Marjory who nearly kissed the ground in front of Rose when she arrived with her daughters at school. That was just after she heard that the new family in the lodge has a toddler and another on the way.'

'You see, you sorted all that out too.

You saved the school from closure.'

'Nonsense. That all happened by the by.'

Steve got up and threw another log on the fire, creating sparks which floated up the chimney like fairy dust. He leaned on the high mantelpiece and looked across at Polly. The glow from the fire cast shadows across his features making him look even more handsome. Polly's heart did a flip.

'You fixed me too.'

Polly gave a nervous laugh. 'Did I? In what way?' She detected a shift in the conversation's dynamics.

'You helped me to regain my confidence. I never thought that would ever happen.' He sat down again and took her hands in his.

'So much so that I've decided to go self-employed.'

Polly sat bolt upright, thinking she'd misheard.

'That's a bold decision.'

'It sort of crept up on me. Through word of mouth half of Izzy's street seem

248

to want my services. I suspect, if it was up to your aunt, she'd have done a leaflet drop by now!

'I've had to turn down work because I can't fit it all in. I'll earn more by working for myself. Does that make me sound ungrateful to the Hall?'

'Not at all. They won't think so, either. I'm so happy for you, Steve.'

'Well, I spoke to Hazel yesterday and explained my plan. She said I can stay here for as long as I wanted.'

'I'm not surprised. She has a generous spirit.'

'So that's my confidence fixed. Let's see, what else? Ah, yes, you taught me how to trust again. That was difficult but, with your influence, I did it.

'The biggest and most amazing thing of all is that you taught me to open up my heart and love again.'

He leaned forward and kissed her lips.

Polly held her breath and wished the curtains were open as she was sure, at that moment, a star was shooting across the sky.

Without warning Steve slipped off the sofa on to the hearth rug, still holding Polly's hands.

Time seemed to stand still and she knew what he was going to ask her. She wanted to remember this moment always and lock it in the recesses of her soul.

'I love you, Polly. Will you marry me?'

She looked at his expectant face through blurred vision.

'Yes, I'll marry you, Steve. On one condition.'

'What's that, my love?'

'That Freya gets to be flower girl.'

He gave a chuckle.

'I think that's the very least she will expect!'

'Good, I'm glad that's agreed. Now to practicalities. Your place or mine? After we're married, that is.'

'I didn't dare think that far ahead — I wasn't even sure you'd say yes.'

'Well, I have said yes. Look, let's forget about the details for now. As Marjory says these things often have away of resolving themselves.'

'Marjory is a very wise woman.'

Polly snuggled further into his embrace.

As she watched the flames dancing in the hearth she indulged herself in dreaming of the long and happy future they would have together.